Advanc
Night of the Living Dead Christian

"Matt Mikalatos gets what the gospel is all about. It's not about reform or spiritual cosmetology. We're dead, we're monstrous, we're enemies of God. But because of his great mercy, he desires a relationship. He wants us to become like him. What that looks like is beautiful, funny, and tragic, and it's captured well in this transformational allegory. Have fun as you read. Enjoy the goose bumps, laughs, and tears."

CHRIS FABRY, *radio host and bestselling author of* Almost Heaven

"Somewhere between classic monster movies and C. S. Lewis is Matt Mikalatos's inventive sci-fi gospel drama, *Night of the Living Dead Christian*. Zombies, werewolves, vampires, mad scientists, crossbows, and . . . *Jesus?* It's all there in this endlessly energetic story about how God's grace can transform every last one of us. But can monsters really teach us about Jesus? Before you laugh at that question, read this wildly creative, surprisingly insightful book."

BRETT MCCRACKEN, *author of* Hipster Christianity: When Church and Cool Collide

"I love to laugh and I love to think. So what a treat it is to find a book like *Night of the Living Dead Christian* that allows me to do both. Often at the same time. In his fun, campy monster book (did I mention I also love monsters?), Matt Mikalatos takes readers on an adventure every Christian needs to take. One that helps us see our own zombie or werewolf or vampire tendencies that make us live like we're dead and one that teaches us to shed those tendencies and live like we've been reborn."

CARYN DAHLSTRAND RIVADENEIRA, *author of* Grumble Hallelujah

"In *Night of the Living Dead Christian*, Matt Mikalatos sinks his comedic teeth into our spiritual jugular . . . only to find us nearly drained of the new life Christ promised. This is a book that disarms with its wit while driving a stake into our spiritual complacency. With the help of werewolves, vampires, and zombies, Mikalatos takes a fun but penetrating look at the quest for spiritual transformation . . . and us monsters who need it most. Five out of five silver bullets!"

MIKE DURAN, *author of* The Resurrection

Praise for Matt Mikalatos
and *Imaginary Jesus*

"Startling, contemporary, meaningful. . . . Mixing questions of suffering and free will with a nexus of weirdness, Mikalatos throws Christian fiction into the world of Comic-Con and *Star Wars*."
    PUBLISHERS WEEKLY

"Think Monty Python meets C. S. Lewis. . . . Rarely does a book slide so easily from the laugh-out-loud moments to the tender-yet-challenging moments."
    RELEVANT MAGAZINE

"Mikalatos's debut work takes readers on a hilarious ride."
    CBA RETAILERS + RESOURCES

"I've found my new favorite book, not only for the insights it offered me but for the conversation it's afforded my church. Mikalatos packages honesty with humor that allows us to ask questions we'd rather not ask, but absolutely should."
    TONY MYLES, *YouthWorker Journal*

"Gutsy, irreverent, hilarious, courageous, poignant, eye-opening, bizarre, quirky, mold-breaking—those are a lot of bold adjectives to describe one little book. But *Imaginary Jesus* deserves every one of them and many more. That's because Matt Mikalatos accomplishes so much in one slim novel that your brain struggles to keep pace with the thoughts that go whooshing through it. . . . Lest you think this is all fun and games, let me assure you that it's not. Matt's encounter with the real Jesus is as compelling a scene as you'll find anywhere in contemporary literature. . . . What a joy it was to find this treasure! I'll take this book over a thousand sermons and a library full of theological tomes on who Jesus is."
    FAITHFULREADER.COM

"[A] sharp-witted, mind-bending, faith-challenging excursion. . . . If Mikalatos's wry wit doesn't pull you into the book within a couple pages, his action-packed chase of Imaginary Jesus will soon have you flipping pages. But be warned. Beneath the excitement of the adventurous chase and the humor of his comic wit, Mikalatos packs some heavy biblical punches that may send your own imaginary Jesus spinning, leaving you to confront the real One."

DC CHRISTIAN FICTION EXAMINER

"Take the theological forcefulness of Bonhoeffer, combine it with the imaginative whimsy of C. S. Lewis and the wit of Charles Spurgeon, and you get Matt Mikalatos. He is a gifted writer, a true Christian, with a first-rate mind. *Imaginary Jesus* is a startlingly original, comedic, and theologically true tour de force. It marks the debut of one of today's most prominent young Christian writers."

GARY THOMAS, *author of* Sacred Marriage *and* Pure Pleasure

"Matt Mikalatos writes like a happy-go-lucky C. S. Lewis. *Imaginary Jesus* is relentlessly funny, with surprisingly profound spiritual insights."

JOSH D. MCDOWELL, *author and speaker*

"If there is such a thing as a holy romp, this is it. I laughed, I applauded and cheered, I thanked God. Every Christian I know will want to read this one!"

PHYLLIS TICKLE, *author of* The Great Emergence

"Matt Mikalatos has written a funny, surprising, gutsy tale. Through his writing, I recognized many of my own false assumptions and shallow beliefs, and possibly even more importantly, I really enjoyed the journey."

SHAUNA NIEQUIST, *author of* Cold Tangerines *and* Bittersweet

"Matt Mikalatos has an incredible gift that is highlighted throughout *Imaginary Jesus*. While this book is hilarious, it will also cause you to stop dead in your tracks and evaluate what you really believe about Jesus. I was convicted over and over at how many times I've created an 'imaginary Jesus' to fit my self-centered, ego-driven, materialistic desires."

PETE WILSON, *author of* Plan B *and pastor of Cross Point Church in Nashville*

"I didn't know what I was getting into when I started reading *Imaginary Jesus* by Matt Mikalatos. By the second page, I was hooked by its humor and challenging insights. Be prepared to have your relationship with Jesus enriched and enlarged by this fun and fascinating look at how we tend to picture Jesus on our own terms."

TREMPER LONGMAN, *Robert H. Gundry Professor of Biblical Studies at Westmont College*

"Like anyone, I suppose, I was wondering what was in store for me as I opened the inaugural book written by an unknown author. As I finished *Imaginary Jesus*, I had a response I had never experienced before. I was astonished! *Imaginary Jesus* not only entertained me to the point that I was embarrassed by my public outbursts of laughter, but it also challenged my faulty thinking on who Jesus was and is. Matt's zany sense of humor was only outdone by the fact that he made so much sense! I'm grateful he let us into his wacky universe!!"

CHRIS ZAUGG, *executive director (Keynote) of Campus Crusade for Christ*

"Crazy and creative and utterly captivating. *Imaginary Jesus* is an entertaining annihilation of all the false and frustrating idols that need to be kicked around a little more."

DALE AHLQUIST, *president of the American Chesterton Society*

"Matt Mikalatos is a crazy man. But he is a wise crazy man. *Imaginary Jesus* is a crazy book. But don't let that fool you. It has a powerful message that is desperately needed for our insane times. So just go with it and let Matt take you on a hilariously serious journey through the oddly firing synapses of his brain. And don't be surprised if you lose some unnecessary baggage along the way."

COLEMAN LUCK, *Hollywood screenwriter, executive producer (*The Equalizer, Gabriel's Fire*), and author of* Angel Fall

"Perhaps the funniest Christian book of all time. Including the future. But more enjoyable if read in the present."

KEITH BUBALO, *national director of the Worldwide Student Network*

"Imaginative, thought-provoking, funny, and especially convicting. This book exposes my own imaginary Jesus, as well as the many others out there. It reads like an updated version of Phillips's *Your God Is Too Small*, only with a lot more wit and creativity. This is the Matt Mikalatos I know—sharp, hungry to know God, passionate to reach a lost world. Matt helps all of us see our own propensity to idolatry and brings us back to the real Jesus."

DR. JOHN E. JOHNSON, *associate professor of pastoral theology and director of the Doctor of Ministry program at Western Seminary; senior pastor of Village Baptist Church in Portland*

"*Imaginary Jesus* is the most powerful and clever book I've read this year. I am already recommending it to everyone I know. Which now includes you. . . . Read it."

LEAD SINGER, *Page CXVI*

"With uncompromising awareness and hilarious creativity, Matt Mikalatos delivers a tour de force that is accessible, entertaining, and thought provoking. You'll laugh out loud at Mikalatos's brilliant humor, but watch out—while you're laughing, he'll hit you square in the jaw with a solid right hook when he presents you with your own mythology about Jesus."

COACH CULBERTSON, *editor of* Coach's Midnight Diner *and coeditor of* Relief Journal

"*Imaginary Jesus* is a fast, wild, unnerving ride. Think J. B. Phillips (*Your God Is Too Small*) on six shots of espresso running crazy through the streets of Portland, Oregon."

DAVID SANFORD, *author of* If God Disappears: 9 Faith Wreckers and What to Do about Them

"When I read *Imaginary Jesus*, I laughed so hard milk came out of my nose . . . and I wasn't even drinking any."

ADAM SABADOS, *just some guy*

NIGHT OF THE LIVING DEAD CHRISTIAN

MATT MIKALATOS

SALT**RIVER**®

AN IMPRINT OF

TYNDALE HOUSE PUBLISHERS, INC.

Library of Congress Cataloging-in-Publication Data

Mikalatos, Matt.
  Night of the living dead Christian / Matt Mikalatos.
      p. cm.
   ISBN 978-1-4143-3880-4 (sc : alk. paper)
   I. Title.
   PS3613.I45N54 2011
   813´.6—dc22   2011020880

Printed in the United States of America

17 16 15 14 13 12 11
 7   6   5   4   3   2   1

To my father, who taught me all a boy needs to know about monsters and many other astonishing things. Thanks, Dad. I love you.

Contents

INTRODUCTION

Monsters do, of course, exist.

Despite our preferences, despite our denunciations and scientific proofs, despite illuminating our porches at night in the vain hope that these brave lights will keep the darkness from our homes, this simple fact remains. I know this all too well, and from common experience. I do not speak of metaphors or children in skulled clothing at Halloween, but true monsters—creatures of darkness who walk among us with impunity and ill intent.

Nevertheless, when our children cry out in the night we hush them and say, "There is nothing to fear" before we triple-check the locks on the doors, before we shut the windows and draw the blinds. We reassure our children that they are safe, despite the fact that we know such assertions to be demonstrably false. We all know that there are pale-skinned creatures in the darkness, and that the howl at full moon is not always the neighborhood dog, and that fear in a world such as ours is a sane and laudable emotion designed to spare us harm.

We prefer Seneca, with his noble *homo homini res sacra,* to the earthy insistence of Plautus that *lupus est homo homini.*

Seneca observes humans treating one another as sacred beings, but Plautus sees us tearing one another apart like animals. Plautus observes the human race more keenly, for we all know in our moments of deepest honesty that human beings, at least some of them, are scarcely disguised wolves dressed in designer clothing. This stubborn refusal to embrace the reality of the world around us is, perhaps, the quintessence of the human experience. Nevertheless, this is the story of one neighborhood much like your own. A neighborhood that I know intimately because—make no mistake—I appear in the pages of this book.

The narrator and my neighbor, Matt Mikalatos, inexplicably styles these events into a comedy, and though I felt nothing but pain at the time, this story is, after all, one that meets the Greek definition of the *commedia*. It is a reminder that despite our monstrous lives, our every story need not be one of tragedy. Which is to say, the missive that follows is not a horror story. It is a mirror. Take courage and gaze into it carefully.

Cordially,

Luther

A concerned citizen and friend of the author

CHAPTER I

WHO ARE THE PEOPLE IN YOUR NEIGHBORHOOD?

MONSTERS DON'T EXIST. I had been telling myself that for nearly a week. But it was the sort of night you could almost believe in them. A bone-white moon hung in a field punctuated with bright stars, and dark clouds moved across the sky like slow-moving barges. It was nearly Halloween, and despite the cobwebs, giant spiders, tombstones, skulls, and electronic screams, it was a pleasant night. But I didn't feel pleasant. I felt nervous. It was a week ago today that I accidentally interrupted the argument between my neighbor and his wife, and since then I had felt jumpy in the neighborhood at night. Nervous. Always looking over my shoulder. But, I told myself, there's no such thing as monsters.

I was on patrol, like every night. My neighbors hadn't shown any interest in starting a neighborhood watch program, so I walked the beat myself, a solid pair of walking shoes on, gloves with no fingers, a pair of binoculars swinging jauntily around my neck, and my cell phone in hand, the numbers 911 already dialed and just waiting for an eager thumb to press SEND. In my other hand I held a long, heavy flashlight for bludgeoning ne'er-do-wells. I couldn't let a little incident like last week's keep me from my appointed rounds.

Up ahead, on the corner of 108th Street in the middle of a cluster of identical houses with the identically perfect lawns that permeated our neighborhood, stood a lanky man in a long white lab coat, a pair of goggles pushed up into his disheveled hair. A thick nest of electrical wires coiled out of a nearby streetlight and into a box he clutched with thin, white hands, and he was laughing and doing a sort of merry jig as I approached, the box squealing and flashing with a riot of handheld casino gaudiness.

"Excuse me," I said. Of course I needed no excuse since it was, after all, my neighborhood, and I was not the crazy person connecting wires to streetlights. But it always pays to be polite. Although when you're a neighborhood watch guy out on patrol, sometimes it also pays to be a no-nonsense guardian of the suburbs. I was just waiting for this guy to give me an excuse to go all "no nonsense" on him. He looked like the kind of guy who probably had too much nonsense in his life, and I was the perfect person to change that.

The man turned to me and grinned. He held the box out

toward me. "No doubt you would like to ask me about the work of inexplicable genius I hold in my hands."

"As a matter of fact, yes." I shifted my stance and held the flashlight nonchalantly over my shoulder, making it clear that I could give him a glancing blow if necessary. "Do you have a permit for that big mess of electrical wiring there, sir?"

His eyes widened, and he tittered nervously. He glanced furtively up the street, then shoved the box into my hands. "One moment." He ran halfway down the street, his lab coat billowing up behind him, and shouted, "Hibbs!"

A gate swung open on the Murphy house, which had been sitting empty for three months. A man came walking from the backyard, easily seven feet tall. His arms and chest were thick where the scientist's were thin, and he gave the impression of a man who had been stuffed full of something, that he held more than blood and muscle and bone under his skin. He wore a tight shirt that showed off his muscles. Stenciled across his chest were the words THE HIBBS 3000. He regarded me coolly.

The scientist grabbed one enormous arm and asked, "Hibbs, do we have a permit for this endeavor?"

Hibbs looked at me and then back at the scientist. "Negative. This power source, which we require for our experiment, cannot be legally accessed, Doctor."

The scientist smiled at me, relieved. "Well, there you have it. Can't get a permit for something that's illegal, now can you?" He snatched the box away from me. "Would you like to watch our experiment, good neighbor?"

"You can't do illegal experiments here in our neighborhood!"

The scientist cocked his head sideways. "Oh. Why's that?"

"It's breaking the law."

"Ha ha. So is speeding, my dear boy. But that doesn't stop anyone." He took my hand and shook it firmly, then chuckled to himself. "So is cloning human beings, ha ha, at least in one's garage, but that never stopped me, no!"

"That's it, pal," I said, and I set my flashlight on the sidewalk and whipped out the tiny little notebook and even tinier pencil I carried in my back pocket, wet the tip of the pencil with my tongue, flipped open the notebook, and put my pencil at the ready. "What's your name?"

The doctor looked at his box, which was humming now. I felt a mild heat coming off of it. "Hibbs, that last electrical boost seems to have done the trick." He jumped, as if his brain had prodded him that I was waiting for a reply, and said, "Oh yes, my name is Dr. Daniel Culbetron. And my associate there is the Hibbs 3000. He's a robot."

"Android," the Hibbs 3000 said.

Culbetron threw one hand up in the air. "Potato, tomato. Don't be so sensitive, Hibbs." He turned to me, as if confiding a great secret. "Robots are notoriously unbalanced emotionally."

Hibbs turned to me, another coil of wire in his hands. "You have yet to exchange your appellation with us."

"I'm Matt Mikalatos, Chief Officer of the local Neighborhood Watch."

The box in Culbetron's hand started warbling and beeping, and he laughed and waved it at Hibbs. "We had best find a safe observation point." He looked over his shoulder, as if he had misplaced something, then over his other shoulder, and then turned in a complete circle, wrapping himself in cords and giving the appearance of a circus clown looking for a small, collared dog. "Where is our benefactor, Hibbs? Do you think he'll want to see our device being tested?"

I tapped the box. "What exactly does this thing do?"

The Hibbs 3000 paused, then looked at me and said, "The apparatus creates a surge of auditory effluvia that is anathema to the lycanthrope."

Dr. Culbetron, midway through unraveling his Gordian knot of electrical wiring, sighed and shook the box at Hibbs. "In English, Hibbs. This poor neighborhood constable cannot possibly comprehend your robotic ramblings." He handed me the box and stepped gingerly over a cord. "It's a device designed to create sounds that will be upsetting to werewolves."

"I don't understand."

"It's quite simple, really. Perhaps you have seen anti-rodent devices that plug into an electrical socket. They produce a series of high-pitched squeals, above the range of human hearing, that drive away mice and some insects. It sends them scurrying out of their little hidey-holes, charging past the devices screaming their furry little heads off as they head for the woods." He snatched the box and held it over his head. "This box does precisely that—for *werewolves*."

I tightened my grip on my flashlight and a chill ran through me. "There's no such thing as werewolves."

Hibbs was setting a ladder up against the side of the Murphy house. "There is a 63 percent likelihood that the device will evoke a similar response from multiple monster species."

"There's no such thing as monsters!"

Culbetron put one hand gently on my shoulder. "Werewolves, of course, are rather rare in this part of the world. You're quite right about that. The vast majority of the lycanthropic population has been confined to Eastern Europe."

Hibbs shook his head. "Scientific research on this topic is irresponsibly scant. Dr. Culbetron does not represent scientific fact with his previous assertion."

"Well then, Hibbs, let us start some scientific research of our own!" With that he and Hibbs pulled earphones on, and Culbetron slammed his palm down on the button in the center of the box. A sound something like a mix between a jetliner, a baby crying, and fingernails on a chalkboard came screaming out of the box.

"One minute and forty-seven seconds, Doctor!" Hibbs shouted.

"Thank you, Hibbs. To the roof! Let the science begin!"

They climbed a metal ladder onto the roof of the Murphy house, Culbetron struggling to ascend with the box in one hand and Hibbs waiting patiently behind him. I put my hands over my ears, and Hibbs fixed me with a curious

look. I shouted at him to ask if they had a third pair of earphones, but he didn't answer. I was about to ask again when
Culbetron shouted from the roof, "Zombies!"

"There's no such thing as zombies!" I shouted back.
I could barely hear him over the horrible shrieking of the
machine. The volume was growing, and the lights in the
neighborhood dimmed.

"Look, Hibbs! Coming from the south—a horde of
the undead! It works, Hibbs! It works!" There was a popping sound from the roof, and sparks came flying out of
Culbetron's box. Startled, he fell backward into Hibbs, who
tried to catch him, and they both stumbled over the apex of
the roof, slid to the edge, and nearly fell before the electrical cords caught on the gutter. The box, however, flew to
the ground and smashed to pieces. The sound, mercifully,
stopped. Culbetron and Hibbs hung from the roof, their feet
dangling thirteen inches from the ground.

I took my fingers out of my ears. I heard a dull roar, a sort
of rumbling echo in my ears. It appeared that Culbetron's
box had temporarily deafened me. I looked to Culbetron,
who was frantically trying to climb back up the electrical wiring and get onto the roof. I could hear him telling Hibbs over
and over that they must get on the roof before the zombies
came. So my hearing wasn't gone after all. Then what was
that strange rumbling sound?

I turned on my flashlight for comfort and walked down
the street, toward the rapidly increasing sound of riot in the
southern part of the neighborhood. I looked back and could

see the two crazy people clambering back onto the roof of the Murphy house. Maniacs.

I had walked half a block when I saw them come around the corner and turn toward me, just one or two at first, lurching out of the shadows and dragging their stiff legs along the sidewalk. But then a few more came, and then more, and then a terrifying conglomeration of people with green-painted faces and torn clothes and makeup that gave the appearance of torn flesh. My finger hovered over the SEND button on my cell phone, but I hesitated. What would I say to the dispatcher? I ran through the conversation in my head. First the operator would ask me the nature of the emergency. I would say zombies. The operator would ask me what the zombies were doing. I would say running around, but that I was afraid they might bite someone. The operator would remind me that this was, after all, America, and zombies are allowed to walk around and that I should call back if the zombies ate someone or a house caught on fire or something. By the time I got to this point in my imaginary conversation, the first zombie had reached me—a fast zombie in running shoes and sweatpants—and he snatched the phone away from me, hit SEND, and shouted into it.

"Hey!" I said, and I grabbed the phone away from him and shut it. "I'm Chief Officer of the local Neighborhood Watch, sir. You can just tell me the nature of your emergency." Looking frightened, the zombie pointed at the horde running up behind him. "Zombies?" I asked. He shook his head furiously and pointed again. "Zombies!" I said again.

"I know. I see them." He shook his head and held up three
fingers. "Three words." He nodded. "First word." The zombie made a terrible face. "Indigestion? No. Bad taste? No.
Wait. Is it . . . monster?" The zombie nodded and held up
two fingers and started running in place. The rest of the zombie horde was almost on us now. "Run? Chase? Chasing?"
The zombie nodded and held up a third finger, then pointed
at himself. "Monster chasing me!" The zombie smiled and
jumped up and down and pointed at my phone. Then he
looked at how close the other undead were to us, gave a little
shriek, and ran away. Zombies were nicer than I thought—or
that one was, at least. The rest of the zombies were starting
to speed past me now.

"Ruuuuuuhhn," one of them moaned. A snapping,
growling sound came from behind it, and I looked past the
zombie-things to see a large, furred creature biting at their
legs and herding them toward me with a ferocious speed.

I stared in wonder at this vicious animal. "Is that . . .
a giant badger?" But before I could get a good look I was
swept up into the tide of the undead. Against my will, my
feet started moving, and the looks of real terror on the zombie faces convinced me I didn't want to get too close to that
angry badger at the back of the crowd. I started pushing
zombies out of my way. I could hear the badger-thing right
behind me now, the snapping of its long, white teeth right
at my heels. One zombie looked over at my scalp and licked
his lips. My wife has always said she loves me for my brains,
which is great, but attractive brains are a real disadvantage

when there are hungry zombies around. I pushed him into a thornbush along the sidewalk, and a panicked laugh bubbled out of my mouth. "Sorry," I said. I wasn't sure whether being polite to zombies pays off or not.

The zombies were starting to scatter now, disappearing by twos and threes down side streets, under hedges, and between parked cars. The badger was getting closer and had a disturbingly wolflike appearance.

"A werewolf!" Culbetron was yelling at me from the rooftop. I kept running, but looking back at the badger I could see now that it was definitely more wolf than badger. It was, in fact, more man than badger too. It was bent over like a man running on all fours, its back twisted down toward canine legs and clawed, furred hands. A fountain of drool was pouring from the creature's fang-studded mouth, and I could tell as it got closer that it was bigger than me. Culbetron cupped his hands around his mouth and shouted, "You should run faster!"

I considered shouting a sarcastic thanks to the doctor, but I was already short on breath, so instead, I took his advice. I could hear the snapping teeth of the wolf getting closer, and the sound of its claws clicking on the sidewalk. I threw my flashlight back at the wolf, but I heard it clatter to the ground and the wolf growled. Then I felt the sudden, considerable weight of a large, clawed mammal settle into my back, and I fell onto the cement, skidding along for several feet before we stopped.

The wolf rolled me over and huffed in my face. Despite my expectations, its breath didn't smell one bit like rotting flesh.

I put my hands on its face and tried to push it back. "Your breath is surprisingly minty." The wolf snarled, a menacing, terrifying sound. A small voice in the back of my head informed me that since the wolf took such good care of his teeth, he should have no problem eating me right up. I let out a low moan and tried to think how to get out of this situation. I felt like I was about to start crying, and the wolf was pushing his gaping maw uncomfortably close to my tasty face. Finally, I gave him the only compliment I could think of: "My, what nice teeth you have." As soon as I said it I regretted it. But I start to babble when I'm panicked, and before I could control myself I said, "Why do you think the wolf in 'Little Red Riding Hood' didn't just eat her in the forest instead of running ahead to Grandma's and waiting there to eat her?" Which, if you think about it, really is an excellent question.

The wolf shook its head, and its yellow eyes narrowed. Its ears perked, and it looked back over its shoulder. It looked quickly back to me just as a straight, silver arrow sprouted from its left shoulder. It let out an animal squeal of pain. I was so startled that I let the wolf fall forward onto my chest, and its muzzle brushed my ear. It snorted, but it almost sounded like it had said a word. Like it had said, "Help." It pushed itself up from my chest, and the look in its face seemed to change from savage hatred to an almost elemental fear. It looked in my eyes one more time, only this time its eyes seemed almost human, as if they were scanning me to see if I might be a source of help, as one soul crying out to another. It was as if the wolf wanted help, not just to escape the hunter, but to escape something inside itself. It jumped from my chest and loped up the street, then catapulted its body over a fence across the street.

I stood up and brushed myself off. My back hurt from the wolf's claws, and my chest hurt from hitting the pavement. The wolf and the zombies had disappeared like sunbaked snow. The neighborhood was quiet again.

A short man with a broken face came charging up the sidewalk, cradling a crossbow in his arms. I realized the silver arrow must have been a bolt from the crossbow. When I say the man's face was broken, that is not an exaggeration. His nose had clearly been broken many, many times, so that he had the unmistakable look of a sheep, and there were scars and lacerations covering his arms and face. Weapons and strange sachets hung from his belt and a bandolier was slung across his chest. He grabbed my arm, and with an intensity that made me enormously uncomfortable he said, "Did the volf bite you?"

"The volf?"

"The verevolf."

"Oh. No. It knocked me down, though." I looked the way the werewolf had come instead of the way it had run off. Something about the look in its eyes after it was wounded made me want to help it, even if it couldn't find the words to ask. "It went, uh, over there."

The man with the broken face shook me, hard. "There are wampires and verevolfs and zombies about. You had best get inside."

Culbetron and Hibbs came running up. A little late, I thought. Culbetron clapped the hunter on the shoulder. "The device worked admirably, sir, did it not?"

"Yah, yah, wery good."

"Until the malfunction," Hibbs said.

Culbetron touched a finger to the broken-faced man's shoulder. "You appear to be carrying a crossbow and a great deal of weapons, Borut."

"Yah. To kill the volf."

Hibbs and Culbetron exchanged glances. "That is antithetical to our purposes," Hibbs said.

Culbetron's face flushed bright red. "We are scientists, sir! Our goal is to capture and study these creatures, and perhaps to cure them."

Borut laughed. "You cannot cure the volf. Here is the only cure." He patted the crossbow cradled in his arms.

Culbetron lifted his nose and said haughtily, "Ours is both a spiritual and a scientific endeavor, Borut. We kill the monsters only as a last resort. This association is finished!"

"As you vish. Now I must find the volf." Borut ran the way I had pointed, the moonlight shining off the cement and glinting on the silver bolt in his crossbow. As he turned the corner and left our sight, a chilling howl came from behind us. Culbetron and Hibbs both turned toward me, looks of wonder on their faces.

"Yeah, it ran the other way. Come on, we have to make sure it doesn't eat my wife and kids!" We ran in the direction of the howl, and I showed them where the wolf had leapt the fence. A pair of yellow eyes glared at us, and a deep-throated growl came from the creature. On the ground I saw the bolt, swathed in the creature's blood. The wolf bared its teeth, then turned and jumped into the next yard over. We ran alongside the fence. The creature seemed to be moving toward my house, but at the last moment it turned and headed west. About six houses down from my house it ran into the backyard, and we followed. The werewolf was getting ahead of us, but I skidded into the backyard just in time to see a flash of fur and an oversized doggie door flapping in the back door. Note to self: never get a doggie door.

"We have to warn your neighbors," Culbetron said.

"I say we leave well enough alone."

"You're the Neighborhood Watch person!"

"Oh, fine." I walked up to the door and pounded on it. "Werewolf in your house, werewolf in your house!" I ran down the steps without waiting for an answer. "Let's get out of here."

But the door had already opened, and I could see the silhouette of a thin man in the doorway—the same man from last week, I thought. "Can I help you?" His voice made it clear he had no desire to help us, that he saw us as an annoyance. I couldn't see his face in the shadows.

I was suddenly struck with the ludicrous nature of what I needed to tell him. "I think a wild animal might have come in through your dog door."

"Our dog just came in. Is that what you saw?"

"Well, I didn't actually see it go in."

"It was our dog. If that's all you have to say, then good night."

"Sorry to disturb you. Good night."

He closed the door without further comment, which seemed a little rude. I rubbed my arms and looked around nervously. "So there's still a werewolf out here somewhere."

"Don't worry," Culbetron said. "We'll help you catch it."

"You'll help me do what now?"

Hibbs interrupted, "Doctor, it appears that the zombies have recovered their equilibrium and once more roam the night seeking to assimilate the living."

I turned to Hibbs. I could see several zombies lumbering up behind him. "When you say 'assimilate the living,' do you mean turn us into zombies?"

"Affirmative."

Culbetron rubbed his chin. "Or eat us. Those are the options when dealing with zombies, to be assimilated or digested."

The zombies were clumping up now, flowing in from around the neighborhood, down streets, under rosebushes, and behind cars, and they seemed to sense the three of us on the sidewalk, because they were headed our direction. "Follow me." I ran down the street on the sidewalk farthest from the zombies, Culbetron and Hibbs close behind me. "My house is just ahead." But when we got to my house, there were three zombies milling around on the porch. They appeared to be stuffing flyers into the handle of my front door. These were very strange zombies. I punched my fist into my palm. "I knew I should have put up a 'No Soliciting' sign." I looked at the other zombies. Now that I noticed it, most of them had bright green flyers in their hands. I picked one up off the ground and read it out loud: "REVIVAL IS COMING. Join us this Sunday for our weekly REVIVAL. The Lord is coming to Dr. Bokor's church. Are you?" The church name and address had been torn off. Weird. I folded it and put it in my pocket.

Maybe the Lord was going to Dr. Bokor's church, but I wasn't planning on being there. I have my own church, after all, and I was pretty sure that God would be there, also. Minus the brain-eating, flyer-leaving parishioners.

Culbetron asked, "What now?"

My neighbor Lara's house was behind us, but there were zombies in our path. I knew she would let us in, but the slow approach of the undead threatened to cut us off. Some of them looked hungry. The choice appeared to be move forward to be eaten or remain where we were. "We could go to my Secret Lair," I said reluctantly. "I usually only go there alone to hatch secret plans where my wife or daughters won't get in the way."

"I suggest we move swiftly."

I pulled my keys out. "Quickly then!" I unlocked the door to my Toyota Corolla and leapt into the driver's seat, slammed the door, and unlocked the back door just in time for Culbetron and Hibbs to crowd in. Their knees were in their faces, but they were safe from the groping hands of the zombies hitting the glass. The zombies looked through the windows at us in uncomprehending confusion.

"Drive!" Culbetron shouted. "Lead us on, sir, to your Secret Lair!"

I cleared my throat. "This is my Secret Lair."

Culbetron looked out the window, where a zombie was absently smashing his palm into the glass, over and over. Hibbs shifted his long legs, which caused both Culbetron and me to rearrange. Culbetron scratched his chin, as if thinking carefully what he should say in response to this revelation. When he finally spoke, he said, "This is the worst Secret Lair ever."

"If it weren't for your earsplitting invention, we wouldn't be in this mess. I guess we just wait here until the zombies move along." But the zombies didn't move along. They gathered around the car and started to push and shove at it.

"We're going to be fine," Culbetron said.

"There is a high likelihood that this will end poorly," the Hibbs 3000 said dispassionately.

"You're such a pessimist."

"It is in my programming." One of the zombies started to smash the rear window with a brick.

Culbetron suggested we drive away, but the Secret Lair was out of gas. A zombie tried the door handle. I started getting nervous. Hibbs counted the zombies outside the car (twenty-seven) and said, "A zombie population of this density in a suburban neighborhood is statistically unlikely."

"A good point, Hibbs 3000. Matt, perhaps you should tell us if you have noticed anything strange in the neighborhood during your patrols."

A zombie crawled up onto the hood. I turned on the windshield wipers to try to get him off, but he grabbed the blades and started chewing on them. "Well. There was this one weird thing a week ago."

More zombies were gathering, and as they pushed on the back passenger door I heard the crunching sound of metal denting inward. "You had best tell the story quickly," Culbetron said.

"Yes, of course. It all started when we heard the screaming . . ."

CHAPTER 2

PROLOGUE

I NEVER KNEW WHAT a bloodcurdling scream sounded like until that moment. I turned to my wife, Krista, who had jumped so high that our popcorn bowl disgorged its contents all over the couch, and said, "I think my blood just curdled" at the same moment that she said, "What was that?"

"A bloodcurdling scream," I shouted as I leapt to my feet.

"Whoa, hold on there," Krista said, grabbing me by the shirt and yanking me back onto the couch. "Where are you going?"

I pointed toward the front door. "Someone's in trouble!"

"Every time you hear a bump in the night you go charging out the door. Don't you think you should stay here and protect your pregnant wife and two daughters?" I considered this. She made an excellent point. That was a strength of hers, that she often made excellent points.

"Yes," I said reluctantly. "Although a compelling argument could be made for taking the initiative to stop trouble before it ever gets to the house."

She grinned at me. "Then again, you are the Admiral of the Neighborhood Watch."

I sat up and looked at her, trying to read her expression. Was she saying I could go check it out? "Chief Officer," I said. I rubbed her belly and felt a strong kick. "Aw, and the little Neighborhood Watch Junior Officer wants to go out too!"

Krista grabbed my hand. "Go make the world safe for us, dear. But try to remember that the girls and I need you here at home, too."

I kissed her quickly and jumped up, heading for the front door. I slammed the door behind me and locked my precious family safely in the house. I heard Krista call after me to be careful, but nine times out of ten when I go investigate a disturbance it's just some neighborhood kids yelling about something. On the other hand, I had never heard a blood-curdling scream in our neighborhood before.

The thing about curdled blood is that you have to get it moving right away or you go into shock. I ran in the direction of the riotous yelling, and I ended up—barefoot and out of breath—seven houses away, standing in a neighbor's driveway. A silver sedan stood idling in the night cold, exhaust floating away like the lonely smoke of

an abandoned cigarette. The front door of the house stood
cracked open, and more yelling came from inside. It was a
woman's voice, tremulous and piercing. I debated knocking, but then I looked down into the car and saw a young
girl strapped into her car seat, a square of yellow blanket
pulled up around her ears, a battered teddy bear wedged
uncomfortably under one arm. She looked at me with the
uncertain terror of childhood, and I smiled at her reassur-
ingly. There was no one outside with her, and I decided to
stand watch until her parents came out.

"Don't you dare tell me you'll change this time," the
woman shouted from inside the house, followed by the
sound of breaking glass, and a low, measured male voice.
The door swung open, and a woman flew down the steps.
She was thin and pretty, and she wore a grey suit that looked
like something a woman might have worn in the 1920s. The
curled, blonde hair framing her face gave her the look of a
starlet, but the puffy red eyes and creases of her scowl made
her look human.

"Are you okay, ma'am?"

She stopped, and a neutral look fell over her face like
a curtain. "I'm sorry our argument disturbed you." She
straightened her jacket and wiped ineffectually at her face.
"Do your family a favor and stay far away from my husband."
She looked back over her shoulder quickly. Her husband
walked out onto the porch then, a thin, pinched man with
a pair of spectacles perched on his narrow nose. She gasped
and pushed past me to open her car door.

I turned my back on the man, putting myself between him and his wife, and I asked her, "Do you need help?"

She laughed bitterly. "No one can help us now." She reached across the open car door and grabbed my wrist. "He's a monster." She shook my arm. "Do you understand what I'm saying to you? A *monster*." She looked over my shoulder and shouted, "There's nothing he can do to change it. But at least we'll be free of him." With that, she jumped into the driver's seat, slammed the door, and jerked the car into gear. I watched the brake lights make an angry red scar down the center of the street.

The man on the porch was staring silently in the direction her car had gone. "Are you okay?" I asked him. He turned slowly to look at me but didn't say anything. In the pale light of the moon his eyes seemed to glow green, like an animal's. He stepped up into his house, his eyes still on me like a junk-yard dog watching a stranger on the edge of his territory, and firmly shut his front door.

CHAPTER 3

ZOMBIES VS. VAMPIRES

JUST AS I FINISHED TALKING about my neighbor's front door, the zombies managed to tear the back door off my car. They yanked Culbetron out like candy from a Pez dispenser and then started in on Hibbs. My hand fumbled on the ignition, and I groaned when the engine failed to catch, the yellow light flashing on, as if the big red needle pointing to the *E* wasn't enough reminder that I was out of gas. Hibbs managed to hold on to the car seat for a long second before the zombies pulled him from the car feetfirst. The last thing he said to me was, "All statistical indicators now point to complete disaster."

I jumped out of the car, determined to face the undead mob on my own terms. Luckily, most of them had swarmed over Culbetron and Hibbs, and I had time to pop the trunk to look for a weapon. In the trunk (or, as I preferred to call it, the Trunk of Mystery) I quickly sifted through discarded papers from work, VHS tapes, and bags of ancient sweaters until I came across a pair of plastic vampire teeth and a flattened black cape from Halloween a year ago. It was better than nothing, and once again I kicked myself for not playing baseball. A baseball bat would come in really handy right now, but other than my brief interest in sumo wrestling I had no sports background. And although my *mawashi* sat unrolled in the Trunk of Mystery, I didn't think it would be much help against the zombies. I turned red at the memory of my first sumo match. It was my fourth most humiliating moment. On the bright side, I really had a feeling of flight when my opponent sent me sailing outside of the circle.

I popped the plastic teeth in my mouth and ran around the car, hoping that zombies were as afraid of vampires as they were of werewolves. A crowd of zombies had pinned Culbetron to the ground, and a small group of them were working on something around his head. I stepped closer, afraid of what I might see. Two zombies held his head still while another was placing earbuds in his ears. A fourth was connecting an MP3 player to the earbuds. Culbetron was fighting them, but there were just too many, at least three zombies on each limb. Hibbs, meanwhile, had been pinned also but wasn't fighting them at all. He stared up at the sky with a vacant look. One of the zombies bit him in the shoulder, and Hibbs winced but otherwise stayed as he was.

I lifted my arms high, making sure the light of the streetlamps caused a creepy shadow to fall across the zombies. The zombies turned slowly, as if by hidden signals, and I bared my teeth and hissed at them. I don't know what I was expecting, maybe that they would run away, but instead several returned to their work on Culbetron while a few others stood and staggered toward me. I knew I needed to ratchet it up a notch. "Boooo, I am a scary vampire!"

They didn't stop walking. I heard a door slam on a house across the street behind me. I waved my arms menacingly. "I'll suck your blood until you're dead!" They didn't stop. "You'll have to sleep in a coffin." I racked my brain, trying to think of other vampire stuff. The zombies kept coming. "You'll be able to turn into a bat and control animals and turn into mist, and you won't be able to cross running water!" Vampires are far superior to zombies. I mean, if you were a zombie and you had the choice between shambling around forever eating brains or turning into a bat and flying around and enjoying the night life and just drinking a little blood now and then, wouldn't you prefer that?

That's when I realized I was doomed. I raised my hands to give it one last try, but when I let loose with a vampire hiss, a sound much louder and more frightening came from all around me, a hiss that seemed to say, "Begone from here or feel my wrath." It was the sort of hiss that scared the living daylights out of the undead, and they suddenly leapt up from Culbetron and Hibbs and dragged their stiff limbs out of my yard and around the corner of the fence.

"Amazing." I spit the teeth out into my hand. I hadn't expected that to work. What a nice surprise not to become a zombie snack. I laughed merrily and pointed at the retreating zombies. "Run, you shambling monstrosities, run! That's right, this neighborhood is protected by the Mikalatos Neighborhood Watch. Think about *that* next time you come looking for some brains." One of the zombies turned and gave me a disgusted look. I threw a rock at him, and it flew about ten feet too high and three feet wide and hit the neighbor's car. "Yeah, there's no brains for you here tonight! Our neighborhood is brain-free!"

The Hibbs 3000 labored to his feet, then helped the dazed Culbetron up from the ground. I put my hands on my hips, grinning and still pleased at my victory over the zombies. I never knew they were so easy to scare away. I waited for Hibbs and Culbetron to congratulate me or thank me or something, but they were both frozen, looking off just behind me. I had that sudden creepy feeling that something truly horrible stood drooling over my shoulder, and with a fear-fueled shout I spun around only to discover my neighbor Lara.

Lara and I had gone to high school together, so it was this weird thing that she lived across the street now. Weird in the sense that I couldn't help but feel a little bit less like an adult when she was around. She had her long, dark hair swept down, and a tight pair of dress slacks on, and a white collared shirt, and a black cape. Her skin looked pale, I assume because she was frightened of the zombies.

"Oh, hey, Lara."

"What's all the racket?" she asked. "I heard this horrible noise in the neighborhood, and then when I looked outside I saw all those people dressed like zombies."

I laughed. "Nothing to worry about. I scared them away by pretending to be a vampire."

Now Lara was laughing too, and I noticed her thin, sharp canine teeth. It seemed a little sad to me that Lara had tried on her Halloween costume a week early, but she was single again and I knew she was lonely and bored sometimes. "You going to be a vampire for Halloween?"

She grinned. "Nah. I'm going to be a pirate."

"What's with the teeth then?"

She blushed. "A vampire pirate."

"Oh. Little early for wearing costumes in public, isn't it?"

Lara shrugged. "I don't know. All those people dressed like zombies did it. And your friends there behind you, one of them is dressed like a mad scientist and the other as a robot."

"I prefer eccentric genius," Culbetron said.

Hibbs pointed a finger at his chest. "Android."

Lara looked Culbetron and Hibbs over carefully. "It seems to me that an eccentric genius is more likely to wear a rumpled sweater and mismatched socks than a lab coat and goggles. I'd say you're a mad scientist."

Culbetron threw up his hands in dismay. "Where do you hear such talk? Britain? Because they're the ones who call people 'mad' all the time, meaning insane. It's not right to call people names, you know. Are you saying I'm mad? Well,

I'm not. And I don't care what anyone says, my time-travel machine will work. Not today, no, but soon!"

I cleared my throat. "Lara, meet Dr. Culbetron. He's a little shaken up after that zombie scare."

"Yes. Well." He looked over the rim of his glasses and gave her a hard stare. "I'm not crazy."

I didn't like the way Lara was looking at him, as if he were a charming child, and that's when I noticed he had a wedding ring on. I pointed it out to Lara and said, "He's married."

Lara smirked at me. "You always think I'm after every man who walks by. I'm not in high school anymore."

Dr. Culbetron looked down his nose at me disdainfully. "I am, in fact, married. I am dismayed to admit that I have misplaced my wife, however."

Lara laughed. "Misplaced her? Like a pair of glasses?"

Culbetron's hands reached up, and his fingers walked across his glasses, as if making sure they were there. "Not quite. I'm afraid she came into my laboratory while I was working on my matter transducer. I may have turned her into audio waves, or possibly some sort of extra-dimensional vibration." He noted my blank stare and then finished, lamely, by saying, "I'm still looking for her."

Lara laughed merrily. "My good doctor, I hope you'll come to visit me sometime." She pointed to her house across the street. "You're always welcome to drop in. I get lonely in that big house, and I'd love to hear about your experiments and your search for your wife. And I could use a laugh now and then." She walked across the street, still laughing to herself, and turned back to wave, grinning.

The three of us stood on my lawn and lifted our hands to wave back.

"I don't like her," Culbetron said.

Hibbs grinned. "Don't be so sensitive."

Culbetron glowered at him. "Regardless, it is time for us to consider the fact that we must deal with your werewolf neighbor. Borut will be trying to kill him, which may be the best solution. But I feel confident that if we can capture him, we will have at least a chance of curing him."

"It sounds dangerous. What if he bites one of us? Won't we turn into werewolves too?"

Hibbs began to walk down the sidewalk. "I shall go to the Murphy house and collect the requisite equipment to kill the werewolf should the probabilities dictate the need to do so."

"Whoa, wait a minute. Are you guys suggesting that we kill my neighbor?"

Culbetron took me by the shoulders. "Take courage, man! We are suggesting a kidnapping attempt before we resort to murder."

My stomach lurched.

Culbetron guided me up to the porch. "But first, let's see if your wife will make us a snack!"

My arms went cold and prickly, and then my legs started to give. The last thing I saw was Hibbs's thick legs, moving like pistons as he walked to the Murphy house to gather the murder weapons.

CHAPTER 4

KILL THY NEIGHBOR

When I regained consciousness I found myself laid out on my couch, the Hibbs 3000 towering over me. He held up a metal briefcase. "I have brought the requisite tools."

I groaned. I had hoped for one brief and shining moment that it was only a dream. I still had mixed feelings about kidnapping and/or killing my neighbor. "But we're not even sure he's the werewolf."

Culbetron snorted. "The only way to know for certain is to bait him and make him angry. Hibbs, show Matt the equipment we've brought." He looked at me conspiratorially. "Now, it may be that some of these weapons are purely the result of legends and myths. Their efficiency is yet to be tested, but I am certain some of them will be useful."

We walked into the kitchen. The Hibbs 3000 set the briefcase on the counter and popped the metal clasps, and the case opened with a sigh. He pulled it open like a giant clam, revealing a collection of ridiculous junk. I took hold of the first piece of equipment and pulled it out.

"It looks like a sharpened broom handle."

Dr. Culbetron smiled. "Precisely. Since my wife is currently in another dimension, or possibly shrunken to the size of an atom, I don't suppose she will mind our turning the brooms into stakes for killing the werewolf."

I dumped the contents of the case out on the counter. There was a compact mirror, two sticks tied together to look like a cross, and a container of garlic salt. "You idiots. This is all stuff for killing vampires." I held up the cross. "You could have at least gotten a real crucifix."

Culbetron shrugged. "Apparently there was a big sale on crucifixes last month, and the store we went to only had Protestant crosses left. Will this still work on werewolves, I wonder?" He hefted the cross in his hand, then took a closer look at the salt. He shook his head and said, "The garlic salt, however, was just poorly done."

Hibbs sputtered and threw his hands in the air. "Because of your erroneous expectation that an android can correctly identify garlic at a grocery emporium. I never purchase garlic. That is a function fulfilled by Jen."

"Who's Jen?"

"His secret shopper," Culbetron said, at the same moment

the Hibbs 3000 said, "Just a computer program with whom I am acquainted."

"His secret shopper is . . . a computer program."

"That's right."

"Who buys garlic."

Culbetron cleared his throat. "She's very talented."

I gave them both a skeptical stare, and they gave one another abashed looks. Clearly I had stumbled onto something they didn't want to talk about. "Regardless, this junk is for killing vampires. A werewolf has to be shot with a silver bullet."

Culbetron snorted again. It was an unpleasant habit of his. "And what makes you the expert?"

I ground my teeth. "I'll show you big dummies." I went upstairs to my bedroom and pulled a box out from under the bed—my trophy box. I carried it proudly down the stairs and plopped it on top of their collection of pitiful anti-vampire paraphernalia. Dr. Culbetron took his glasses out and perched them on his nose, and the Hibbs 3000 leaned in close. I could practically hear their big brains whirring. "This is why I should be in charge of any monster hunting we do."

I dumped the contents of the box out on the counter. Hibbs reached over and carefully picked up the two sharpened teeth that had clattered to the counter. He held them up to his eyes and studied them. "Vampire eyeteeth?"

"That's right."

"They're rather small."

I cleared my throat. "Yes. Well. The vampire in question was only about nine years old."

Hibbs narrowed his eyes and looked at me. "You killed a little boy vampire?"

"Man, I never said I killed him. I just yanked his teeth so he couldn't suck blood anymore. It was like a visit to the dentist."

"Impressive," Dr. Culbetron said, holding up a roll of ancient cloth. "It looks as if you've defeated a mummy. Although judging from the amount of cloth here, it must have been a tiny one."

I coughed and snatched the cloth from him. "It was more like a mummified hand. But I did defeat it. Just like this were-creature." I held up the pelt.

Hibbs and Culbetron exchanged looks with one another and then Culbetron said, "That's from a . . . werewolf, is it?"

"No," Hibbs said. "Clearly something smaller."

Culbetron looked uncomfortable. "I hate to hurt your feelings, Matt. But is that a were- . . . badger?"

"Why would you say badger?" I asked, remembering with a shiver my first sight of the werewolf.

Culbetron shrugged. "Because they are creatures of unmatched savagery."

"The diminutive size suggests a mammal of smaller stature," said Hibbs.

"It's a squirrel, all right? A were-squirrel."

Hibbs snickered and put his hand over his face. Culbetron seemed perplexed. "I don't understand. Does it howl at the moon? Was it previously a person? Does it bite people? What does it eat?"

I slammed my fist on the counter. "The point is that I've actually dealt with these creatures before. And I'm telling you that if we're going to kill a werewolf, then we're going to have to use silver bullets, not stakes and garlic salt."

"Very well, you're the expert. But I must understand this were-squirrel phenomenon. It attacks on the full moon?"

I sighed. "No. When a were-squirrel gets nervous it starts chattering a lot and telling jokes and jumping in trees and, uh, causing a lot of distractions."

"Why would you kill that?"

I waved my hands in the vaguest possible motion and shouted, "It's a long story! Suffice it to say that I have vast oceans of experience in this area while you two have absolutely none, and it's time for you to do as I say instead of what seems right to you!"

Hibbs narrowed his eyes. "My impeccable memory reminds me that you accosted us on the street claiming that there is no such thing as monsters. And yet this box of evidence suggests an extensive history with them."

I sighed. "There's a difference between full-fledged monsters and this sort of small-scale freak. I mean, we all have little mutations, but that doesn't mean we're monsters, does it?"

Culbetron and Hibbs exchanged glances. "What do you mean, we all have mutations?"

"Well, for instance, I have an extra half of a vertebra in my back. It's a mutation. I'm a mutant, just like the X-Men.

It's a freakish deviation from the norm, but it doesn't make me a full-fledged monster." I pointed at the collection of odd artifacts in the box. "These are the same sort of thing."

Culbetron scratched his head. "An extra half a vertebra would not make you particularly useful to the X-Men."

Hibbs chimed in, "However, the aforementioned mutant association accepts students into their educational program on the basis of mutation rather than usefulness."

"But what would his superhero name be, Hibbs? Backache Man? He's completely incompetent as a superhero."

I crossed my arms and glared at Culbetron. "Listen, pal, these trophies might be from freaks and mutants more than monsters. But the only thing you've accomplished so far is to flood my neighborhood with zombies and werewolves. If you add in the thousands of hours I spent in my youth watching monster movies and reading comic books, I have a doctorate in monster hunting, while I'm guessing you're still in second grade. So what's it going to be? The Neighborhood Watch way or the highway?"

Culbetron and Hibbs exchanged looks and shrugged. "So. What is the plan, O Wise Monster Hunter?"

I grinned. It had been a while since I had won an argument. "First we get some silver bullets. And then I will reveal my plan to you."

CHAPTER 5

FULL MOON, I SAW HIM STANDING ALONE

PURCHASING SILVER BULLETS at the last minute is ridiculously difficult. No, really. Give it a try. We couldn't find a place to buy them. It was like the entire gun and ammo industry had never considered the possibility that werewolves might attack and we would be woefully unprepared. Culbetron pointed out that this was a clear disadvantage to the human race and that at least if vampires were attacking we could just whittle down our brooms and stake them in the heart. I think this was an attempt to remind me that he had destroyed his wife's brooms in good faith and that he really wanted to use them or he would feel he had wasted getting yelled at in the future for destroying the brooms. Anyway, we decided to make our own silver bullets.

Making silver bullets is harder than I imagined, and frankly neither Culbetron nor the Hibbs 3000 were much help. Our inability to find a source of silver on short notice nearly caused our entire plan to collapse. I briefly flirted with the idea of my wife's jewelry case, but I'm simply not that stupid, regardless of what anyone else might say to the contrary. It was eventually agreed that we would use pre-1964 quarters and dimes, which have a high silver content.

We tried to melt them, which was a complete fiasco. You can't get a pot on your stove hot enough to melt a pile of coins. I stirred the pot with a wooden spoon, but the coins didn't even turn red from the heat. Of course I reached in with my fingers to see how hot they were, and yes, I burned my fingers. Krista kept walking into the room, shaking her head, and walking out again. I hadn't fully explained what was going on. *My love, I'm melting down coins to make bullets so we can shoot the neighbor when he turns into a werewolf.* No doubt she would start asking difficult questions like, "Are you crazy?" or "What are you going to use to mold the molten silver?" or "Did you hear me tell you not to kill the neighbor?" or "Did you think to buy gunpowder?" or "Should I call the ambulance now or later?" My wife is a good question asker.

So is the Hibbs 3000. Soon after I had bandaged my fingers and stood staring angrily into the hot-but-nowhere-near-boiling pot of silver, I suggested moving the coins into the oven, thinking we could melt them in there. Hibbs scratched his head and said, "Perhaps you are unaware that the melting point of silver is 1,763.474 degrees Fahrenheit."

He looked at the knobs on my stove. "This oven appears to be insufficient." I screamed in frustration. Hibbs cocked his head and looked at me quizzically before saying, "Also, do you possess a gun to use once the bullets are manufactured?"

I did not, in fact, have a gun. I retreated to the Secret Lair and hatched a new and ingenious plan. After the coins cooled, I shared my plan with the boys. "First, we spread out around the werewolf's house with our silver coins." We all nodded.

"How does a group of three surround a house?"

"Good grief, Hibbs, I'll draw you a map if you need it."

Culbetron laughed. "Ha ha. Stupid Hibbs. Also. Since we have no guns, how will we deliver the killing blow with the silver?"

I grinned and held my hands up, revealing our secret weapons. "Slingshots for everyone. We use one of the tall evergreens in back of his house to set a snare that will drag him backwards, hang him upside down, and encase him in a fishing net."

"Then we 'soften him up' with this," Culbetron said, hefting a baseball bat over his shoulder. "It's silver," he said proudly.

"Aluminum," Hibbs said nonchalantly, without even having the decency to look at it.

"It's silver *colored*," Culbetron said.

I motioned impatiently for silence. "After we soften him up we'll interrogate him and make sure he's a werewolf. Then you can do your experiments on him. Oh, and this goes without saying, but . . . please don't tell anyone that we kidnapped my neighbor. If it comes to that."

"We'll need some bait," Culbetron said. "A big steak or something."

"I have some ground beef in the fridge."

"It would be logical for Matt to ring the doorbell," Hibbs said.

"WHAT?"

Culbetron tapped his chin and nodded. "Someone has to ring the doorbell. How else can we make sure he comes in the front yard?"

"But—"

"And you are the experienced monster killer with a sea of experience."

"But—"

"And," Culbetron said, with an air of finality. "He's your neighbor."

Which is how I ended up standing on my neighbor's front lawn in the middle of the night, flanked by the Hibbs 3000 with a slingshot. Culbetron was waiting in the backyard with the baseball bat. My heart was trying very hard to claw its way out of my rib cage. The full moon glared down. I marched up to the door, past the sign, which said, "No Halloween Here, Happy Reformation Day!" Great. Apparently the werewolf was a Lutheran. Now I really felt intimidated. I willed myself to ring the doorbell.

A trembling finger answered my call and zeroed in on the bell. Would a werewolf answer the doorbell? Dr. Culbetron assured me that my neighbor's many years of habitually answering the door would cause him to open it even in his wolf state. Hibbs said that the werewolf would probably say, "May I help you?" right before eviscerating me. *Ding-dong.*

I waited for the scrabbling sound of claws on hard wood inside, but instead heard the clumping of dress shoes walking toward the door. The lock made a rattling noise as it was disengaged. The door flew open, and there stood . . . a quite ordinary-looking man. He wore slacks and a button-down shirt, spectacles, and a scarf not unlike the stylish scarf I myself was wearing.

"You," he said.

"Hi."

He waited for a moment. "Well, what is it?"

"Um," I said. "You called me over here."

"I don't even have your number." I looked out into the neighborhood and shrugged. Culbetron was trying to draw a bead on him with his slingshot, but the shot was too difficult with the werewolf and me so close to the house.

Sudden inspiration hit. "I wanted to tell you that I saw some punk kids hanging around here tonight. I think they put something in the grass."

His eyebrows held a meeting above his nose and decided to make him look angry. "Let's have a look." I followed him out into the front lawn. He crouched down over the pile of ground beef. "It's raw meat."

"Does it smell good?" I asked hopefully.

"What's this?" he asked, moving aside the cut grass that

covered the rope in the trap. He pulled on the rope experi-
mentally, then gave it a serious tug. "It's tied to a tree in my
backyard," he said. Great Caesar's ghost, I was in trouble
now. The plan wasn't working. The trap didn't spring. The
guy was yanking mightily on the rope now, but he wasn't
hanging upside down from a tree. He stood up and glared at
me with a strange look in his eyes. He licked his lips.

"FIRE! FIRE! FIRE!" I shouted, and a rain of silver nick-
els, dimes, and quarters engulfed us. They hurt like crazy as
they careened off my body, and I tried to cover my face and
stumble out of the line of fire. I felt my foot sink into something soft, and I looked down to see that I had stepped in an
impressive pile of raw ground beef.

The rope snapped tight around my ankle, and I was
knocked to the ground and whipped into the backyard,
where I found myself hanging upside down in a closely
woven net. Great. At least no one was pelting me with coins
any longer. I could hear my neighbor yelling at Hibbs on the
front lawn. Then I heard something else. A sort of enraged
war cry. I struggled to get a clearer view of my surroundings
just as I heard Culbetron yell, "WOLF PIÑATA!"

"CULBETRON, WAIT! IT'S M—*oof!*"

Immediately followed by, "*Ungh!*"

"*Uhnf!*"

"You softened up yet, wolfboy?"

"Yes," I said weakly.

"Don't smart off with me," he said, and he hit me again.
Then I heard a terrifying growl, and as my net rotated I

saw my neighbor the werewolf running toward us from the front yard, now unmistakably lupine, his teeth bared and eyes flaring with anger, his scarf flying out behind him and his spectacles shimmering in the moonlight. "Run," I said to Culbetron. He turned and saw the wolfman, dropped his bat, and ran.

The wolf loped after him a little way, then came back to where I hung. He picked up the bat in one furred hand and poked me with the tip of it. The net swayed back and forth in front of him.

"If you could not swing it," I said hopefully. "I get motion sickness."

He snarled at me, his green eyes reflecting the moonlight. His red tongue flickered over his glinting teeth. With a quick flick of his claws he cut the net down from the tree, and then he dragged me across the lawn and toward his house, growling all the way.

AND NOW, A WORD FROM OUR WEREWOLF

He likes to make jokes. He turns everything into a farce because, I suppose, he cannot look straight into the difficult eyes of what we are, what we have become. When I write "we" I assume that you understand that I am referring to him, to you, to me, to all of us. It is not to say that I dislike being a monster, being a creature of the night, because God knows that there are many nights when I crave that sudden infusion of air, that falling away of the higher functions and the sharpness that comes with listening to my instincts, with doing what my body tells me to do. The feeling of wind in fur cannot be replicated. The power in my legs when I hunt prey, the simplicity as the chaotic rainbow of our world fades to so many shades of grey cannot be overstated. There is also the moon to consider, how she pulls the tides within men and causes our hearts to swoon at the realization that our role in the universe is not a question to be considered, that there is no question to be considered other than why we deny for even one moment our true nature, why we would fight for even one glorious second the messages that come from our deepest selves and tell us to run, to howl, to fight, to leap, to snarl, to live! There is that part of me that pities those who say the wolf must be tamed.

There is another voice within me as well, one that does not howl at the moon and truly might never howl for any reason whatsoever. This is the voice of the man who is horrified not by the freedom that is represented by the wolf, but by the boundaries that are crossed, the fences that are skirted, the civilities that are ignored or more often laughed at and smashed. His is the voice that says, "I cannot believe I have done that to my wife, and I must find a way to stop myself." It is a tortured voice, one full of horror and guilt and shame.

I have heard it said that if we could find it within ourselves to reject our cultural programming—all the religion and government and social norms that dictate our morality—then we, like our Stone Age ancestors, could be free of guilt at last. We could shuck ourselves of guilt like lizards shucking their skin. It is a pleasant fiction, and one I have often considered, even cherished. The only problem being that every Stone Age tribe we discover passionately desires a solution to the same conflict within themselves. They kill, then seek rituals to cleanse themselves of blood guilt. They steal, and hide what they have stolen. They lie, and lie about their lying. They heed the wolf call within themselves, and fear it, and loathe it, and love it. They are, in a word, human. Or at least as human as we are.

The pain tears like glass in the intestines. Why can I not control this anger? Furthermore, why do I find excuses to become angry, why do I love the feeling elicited by the fear in my wife's eyes? When I become the wolf, why is my last coherent thought how good it feels to let my humanity slip away? It is like an itch that should not be scratched, but if one ignores it, if one does not scratch it, the need to scratch only grows and calls to you until it is all one can think about, and this certainty pounds in one's head that if only for one bright moment this itch could be scratched then perhaps this time the itch would be gone forevermore. So we scratch ourselves until we bleed, and we tear at those around us.

Mikalatos, with his silly stories and ridiculous jokes, cannot say these things. But he feels them. I know this, because we all feel them. There is this tiny, flickering light in the deep darkness, which tells me that all is not as it should be. That I could be something more than this, if only I could find the right path, if only I could find the right fuel for that flickering flame to make it more than a whispered candle's breath. The flame tells me that I am not quite human yet, that I remain a monster. As Oscar Wilde said, "We are all in the gutter, but some of us are looking at the stars." What I am saying, what I am trying to communicate, is that there are disparate moments when even the wolf notices the stars and desires something more than blood, and night air, and the hunt.

It is not a joking matter. It is deadly, for as the fairy tales tell us, the wolf dies in the end. By rifle or axe or fire, the wolf who remains a wolf must find himself breathing his last unfettered breath in the midst of what he does best—biting at those around him. None of us desire to remain wolves. All of us desire to remain wolves. It is the nature of the werewolf to be both man and wolf, and for many years I was satisfied—no, pleased—to be both man and wolf. I could control the wolf, I thought. I could best it with willpower. I carefully constructed rules within our family to show which actions were safe and which ones dangerous. But the canny wolf skirts such rules, and at last my wife wisely stormed out with our daughter. I stood alone, watching our car leave down our street, and wondered if the car was hers now, and the road mine, and perhaps there was nothing left that belonged to us both, other than our history. The wolf had come between us at last and stood demanding either my loyalty or my rejection. I could not leave the wolf.

I misspoke when I said I stood alone watching that car, though the feeling of loneliness descended on me as heavily as the unending weight of the sky. My neighbor Matt Mikalatos had been the lone witness to my final moments with my wife and daughter, and now I wondered if he suspected my true nature. I considered reaching out to him for help. I had read his novel, and I knew he put at least some thought into spiritual things. A happy bonus would be that, should he choose to share my secret with others, no one would believe him, because his novel was filled with ridiculous antics and unbelievable adventures. Should he attempt to share my story he would be, quite literally, the author who cried wolf.

In truth, I suspect I could have found better help, but not nearer. I had rejected any spiritual answer to my dilemma long ago, but I kept circling around the question of Jesus like a wolf circling treed prey. I knew Mikalatos to be one of those people who would constantly come back to the inane and intangible spiritual as an answer to my concrete and physical problems, but with my wife gone I could not help clutching at the nearest possible lifeline. Sickness and nausea gripped me, and I thought it possible—not probable—that help could come from such an unlikely source. I was dying. What had I to lose?

CHAPTER 6

IN THE WOLF'S CHAIR

I WOKE UP TIED TO A CHAIR. A pretty nice dining room chair made of some sort of carved, dark wood. The way the rope was biting into my arms, I knew it must be scuffing up the wood and realized that the werewolf's wife was not going to be happy about this. But then again, maybe your wife is more understanding about such things if you're a werewolf and you've captured a werewolf killer. Or kidnapper. Wolfnapper?

Directly to my left was Hibbs, also tied up, and Culbetron was on my right. He was gagged, so I could only assume that he had been awake when the werewolf captured him. He could prattle on. So the werewolf had caught us all. We had underestimated his wolfy speed.

"Pssst. Hibbs. Use one of your robot gadgets to cut through the ropes."

"I do not have any."

"Shhh! Whisper. You don't have a blade that slices out of your arm or something?"

"No."

"Laser eyes?"

"My apologies, but no."

"Can you heat up so hot that the ropes will catch fire?"

"No, nothing like that."

I sighed. "You are the worst robot of all time. You don't even look like a robot." I glared at Culbetron. "I blame you, you know."

"Mm-mmph," Culbetron said and tipped his head toward the kitchen doorway.

I paused and listened. I could hear the werewolf in the next room, scuffing about. I had a sudden vision of him coming in and biting my head. I don't know why my head, but it just seemed like a werewolf might start at the top and work his way down. I started thumping my chair toward the front door and then heard a sharp intake of air from the other room. My neighbor walked in, wiping the lenses of his glasses with a cloth. He smiled thinly.

"Are the ropes tight enough?" he asked politely.

I flexed my muscles, and there was no give. "Yes, thanks."

"I'm sure you're surprised to see your friends. They tried to abandon you, you know."

I tried to shrug but couldn't. I settled for raising my

eyebrows. "I don't expect them to hang around and be devoured by a ravenous werewolf."

He chuckled. "Is that what you think? That I roam the neighborhood looking for people to eat? If only it were so simple." He pulled over a chair and sat in front of me. "Don't you think it would have been in the news if human carcasses started appearing in the neighborhood?"

Now I felt stupid. This was a fair point. "On the other hand," I said, "the rise of the internet and the fall of the newspaper has led to a serious shortage of in-depth reporting."

My neighbor paused and considered this carefully. "A good point," he said grudgingly. I smiled. My wife got the *New York Times* every day, and I often read the headlines to give me the appearance of a strong native intelligence.

He sat across from us and smoothed the tablecloth. "Where did you find a mad scientist? Or anyone who believes in werewolves for that matter."

"I'll never tell you."

"The bottom of a cereal box?" he said with a healthy dose of disdain.

"Yeah, I found them in a box of Honey Nut Wolf Smashers." I hoped he wouldn't notice that my comment sounded like an insult but didn't actually make a lot of sense.

He sighed and scooted back from the table. "It appears that you are less than advantaged mentally. And yet you somehow learned of my, ah, condition."

"Condition? Are you sick or something?"

"No. My, ah, disability."

"Oh." I tried to give him a knowing look, but I succeeded only in a muddled silence.

"Good grief, man, my lupine attributes." I gave him a tentative smile. "I turn into a wolf when I'm angry," he snapped.

"Oh," I said. "That. Yeah. Figured that out, no problem."

He sighed. "I had hoped that you would be some sort of release for me. But now I see that you are nothing but a savage imbecile."

"Not all that savage if it makes you feel better," I said helpfully. "I have to work at that part of it."

"Well," he said as he started to untie my ropes, "I can't see how you will harm me, unless it's by pure inept accident. I suppose I should let you go. You can't hurt me any more than you could help me."

I rubbed my arms and could feel them coming back to life. "Man, you're good at tying ropes. What sort of help do you need, anyway?"

He narrowed his eyes. "I had hoped you might have some insight about the possible transformative effect of being a follower of Jesus." He nodded to the table behind him, and I saw a copy of my novel, *Imaginary Jesus*, sitting on the table.

I rubbed my arms where the ropes had been biting into them. "Oh, you want me to teach you about being a Christian?"

"I've been a Lutheran my entire life. What makes you think I don't know about being a Christian?"

I shrugged. "Maybe it was when you said you wanted to know about the transformative effect of following Jesus?"

He laughed. "If claiming to be a Christian meant personal transformation, our world would be a far different place. As it is, I know far too many Christians who are worse men as Christians than they were as pagans."

I started loosening Hibbs's ropes. I didn't quite understand what my neighbor was getting at. "So. You're a Christian, but you want to know about transformation. I don't get it."

He rubbed his shoulder. "As it happens, I am not a Christian. A Lutheran, yes, but not a Christian. I know that you claim to be one, and from your book that you claim to have some spiritual insight. I honestly see little evidence of it in this conversation."

Hibbs lifted a finger and butted into the conversation. "Lutherans are, of course, Christians. And are, in fact, well known in many theological circles for having a very tight, neat theology."

The werewolf let loose a low and rueful laugh. "And is that your definition of a Christian? Someone with a tight, neat theology?"

Hibbs processed for a moment. "No. Of course a theology could be tight, neat, and not-Christian. That is to say, any religious belief entails a certain amount of theology. Buddhism is a theology but is not a Christian theology."

"Precisely," he said. "I have been praying for a way to get rid of this curse once and for all. It's all but ruined me. And I thought your Christianity might be an answer. But if you are an answer to my prayers, then God is indeed capricious and cruel. Instead of the three wise men he has sent me the three stooges."

I started on Culbetron's ropes. I decided to save his gag for last, because, well, I shouldn't say why. But it was because I didn't want him to say anything.

"I know it looks bad, but the whole reason we were trying to capture you was to cure you. If you want to talk about spiritual things, if you think that will be helpful, then I'd be glad to do that. I can say, werewolf or not, that God cares about you. Even if you're a non-Christian Lutheran, whatever that means."

My neighbor slumped onto the table. "I should not expect that God should care one whit for one such as me, an apostate monster."

"You're Lutheran," I said. Not a question.

"Yes, of course. And you?"

"Generic Christian. Nondenominational." I held out my hand to him. "My name is Matt Mikalatos."

He glanced over at my book on the table and sighed. "Clearly I already know your name. My name is Luther Martin."

"Martin Luther?" I asked.

CHAPTER 7

"NO, LUTHER MARTIN."

MY NEIGHBOR MASSAGED his temples in frustration. I could see his teeth sharpening, but then they rounded out again and he looked at me with a strained patience. "My father," he said, "was a staunch Lutheran. My elder brother, Marty Martin, walked away from the faith. Haunted by his failure, my father decided that he would give me no choice. And so when I was born, years later, he named me Luther Martin."

"Couldn't you go by your middle name?"

"Of course he thought of that. Which is why my middle name is Anne."

"So you would have a girl's name if you changed your name."

"Correct. As well as the fact that my name is Luther Anne. Lutheran, you see."

"Your father was a strange man."

"Believe me, I haven't told you a tenth of his story. He was an infuriating man, but he would punish me severely if I ever walked one step out of line. So I learned to hide my anger until I couldn't any longer. Which is how I lost my wife."

"It seems careless to lose an entire person," I said.

He pulled open his curtains and looked down the street. "Sometimes I hear a car and think it might be her coming back." His glasses reflected the streetlamps, and the flat blue light spilled into the house and made everything seem cold and distant.

After a long silence I asked, "Why did she leave?"

He leaned his head against the window. "I met Clarissa in college, in German class. She was beautiful. And brilliant, too. She was writing a discourse on the precise parabola described by the ink pot thrown by Martin Luther when he hurled it at the devil. According to her calculations, his throw was the perfect exorcism and could be used to cure all sorts of spiritual maladies. Of course we fell in love. And after several years of trying, we had a daughter. We named her Renata."

"That's a beautiful story," I said.

"The girl cried at all hours of the night. I couldn't sleep. My wife, Clarissa, couldn't sleep either. As our fatigue increased, so did our fights. Little snapping comments at first, and then full-voiced arguments. Until, a week ago, she accused me of not listening to her when she asked me to take out the trash, and I was absolutely enraged. I spilled the garbage across the floor and cursed her soundly. When she tried to calm me I—" His voice caught in his throat. He looked at me defiantly. "It is safe to say that she was right to leave. She gathered Renata and left."

"You frightened her?"

"Indeed. I frightened myself, for that matter. There is no one to call. My father has long since disowned me because of my conduct. He doesn't seem to understand how to tame this raging beast within me. I've prayed for help but to no avail. Until you came along, that is." He blew out a long breath. "I need you to kill the wolf," he said. "Destroy it so that my wife and daughter can return to me and I won't ever harm them."

I thought of my own children and Krista and what it would be like to reach a level of anger where I would harm them, and I couldn't imagine it. I wondered what Luther had done, exactly. And I felt pity for him, that he would know God (or so it seemed) and yet not be able to experience change in his life regarding this anger issue. "I'll help you," I said impulsively.

With a solemnity that only a Lutheran can muster, he thanked me gravely and profusely. "And what is our first action?"

"I think we should start by going to church," I said.

"I went to church my entire childhood," he said. "It's one of the key reasons that I am not a Christian."

"You told me they didn't have answers for you. And this

is our proud Protestant tradition: If one church isn't working for you, find another one. Or make your own."

"Hold on here, one moment," said Culbetron, finally pulling his gag out of his mouth. "I have a thing or three to say here. One, it hurts my feelings enormously that you would gag me and not these others. Two, it's a bit of British stereotyping to call me a 'mad scientist.' You live in America, you might at least say, 'insane researcher' or 'unbalanced scientist' (though I would certainly prefer 'incomprehensible genius'). Three, I am not satisfied with how you keep saying you are Lutheran but not Christian. This displeases me, and I should like you to explain yourself this minute."

"Certainly. One, your feelings are of little importance to me. Two, while your assumptions about the origins of the phrase 'mad scientist' are doubtless correct, it seems to me that you fit the stereotype quite well. You have crazy hair, spectacles, and a white lab coat. You are part of a group of people trying to capture a werewolf. With slingshots. And I wouldn't be surprised at all to learn that you are experimenting with lightning and chemicals to bring some dead creature to life."

"Time travel," Culbetron said, offended. "I'm working on time travel."

"Three, I simply do not believe that a creed or set of beliefs is sufficient to define whether a person is Christian or not. Thus the world is full of people who are Catholic, but not Christian. Evangelical Free, Assemblies of God, Greek Orthodox, or generic nondenominational, but not Christian. Baptist, but not Christian."

"Southern Baptist or American Baptist?" I asked.

"Belief is certainly enough of a definition," Culbetron said.

"I must side with Culbetron," Hibbs said.

"I agree," said me.

"Very well. Then give me your definition of what it means to be Christian."

The three of us instantly scooted our chairs around to form ourselves into what evangelicals refer to as a small group discussion. Culbetron went first. "Let's tell him about how he is going to Hell if he is not a Christian."

Hibbs raised his eyebrows. "Your definition of Christian is 'someone who gets into Heaven'?"

Culbetron shrugged. "I'm not sure I like him, and I just wanted to make sure he knows that I think he's going to Hell."

"Fair enough. Matt, what is your opinion on this matter?"

"We need to have a certain amount of theological weight behind us. I think something like, 'A Christian is someone who believes that Jesus is fully God, fully man, and was sent by God the Father to die on the cross for sinful people as a substitutionary atonement so that they could have eternal life and live forever with God.'"

"That's pretty good."

"A good start, anyway." We labored for hours over this thing. The werewolf lent us some paper and pens. We scribbled things out. We added things in. We tried to make more accessible versions in case he couldn't understand the theological words, and then we remembered he was a Lutheran and we added them back in. I wished mightily for access to the internet, as I was almost certain that Wikipedia could answer all my questions without my having to think at all. But Luther said that he would sooner throw his computer into a slow-moving lava flow than let me touch it.

In the end, I realized that being a Christian was hard to define. Sort of like trying to make silver bullets. I had this feeling that it would be easy, but when I actually got down to attempting it, I couldn't get it right. Eventually Hibbs suggested we just go give it a try and see what happened.

I started us off with a surefire winner. "A Christian is anyone who claims to follow Jesus."

Luther steepled his fingers and looked at us carefully. "I see. You realize, of course, that according to your definition, 75 percent or more of the American populace is Christian."

We stared at him dumbly until Culbetron kicked me under the table. "Uh . . . sure. Yeah, we know that."

"You realize, also, that according to your definition, people like Adolf Hitler would be Christian."

"WHAT?! No way. Hitler was an atheist."

"On the contrary, Hitler was firmly opposed to atheism. He claimed to be a Christian."

At this point Culbetron put his chin in his palm and looked out the window, and Hibbs was studiously cleaning his nails. So they had abandoned me once again. "It's not really fair to use Hitler in an argument, you know. But I would like to revise my definition to say, 'A Christian is anyone who claims to follow Jesus. Except for Hitler.'"

"What about Cortez?"

I stared at him dumbly. "You mean Marc Cortez, my seminary professor? I'm pretty sure he's a Christian."

"No, you dimwit, I mean Cortez who wiped out the Aztecs."

"Oh. He was Catholic."

"You don't count Catholics as Christians?"

"Well. Yeah. I guess I do."

"How about the founders of the Ku Klux Klan? They were good Protestant boys."

"Uh. You can add them to the list with Hitler."

"But they meet your definition, you see. And I do not, because, as you may recall, I said that I am not Christian. Regardless of my beliefs about Christ."

I leaned back in my chair and kicked at Hibbs and Culbetron. "How about a little help here, guys?"

"Right," said Culbetron. "I think what we're missing in the definition is this. First, it requires a certain set of beliefs. Jesus loves humanity, he came to die on the cross for our sins, he rose again on the third day. But, second, we can know him and be in relationship with him only if we truly believe and accept his sacrifice. So a second aspect of becoming a Christian has to do with being 'born again.'"

"I said a prayer, once upon a time," my neighbor said. "And yet . . . I am not a Christian. I want nothing to do with them."

"Why do you keep saying you're not a Christian?" I asked. "I don't get it."

"Because I'm a werewolf," he snapped. "Because I am

NIGHT OF THE LIVING DEAD CHRISTIAN

vicious and violent and uncontrollable. And there is no hope for me, no cure, no salvation. I believed once but I do not believe now, and I cannot be saved."

I cleared my throat. "I think you should try going to church," I said. "Just try it with us."

Luther Martin smiled, but it was a smile that seemed to hide mischief and perhaps evil intentions. "I will take *you* to church," he said. "And I will show you why I am not a Christian."

A WEREWOLF SHARES HIS THOUGHTS ABOUT FATHERS

There is a reason that on Mother's Day the pastor's sermon is about how we do not appreciate our mothers, and on Father's Day the sermon is about how fathers are not living up to the expectations of their role. The male creature is singularly unfit for fatherhood, and in my youth I often found myself wishing I had been born into a culture in which the father abandoned his family once it was sufficiently peopled.

My father's expectations were, I have learned in retrospect, uncommon, but at the time all fathers had unreasonable expectations, or so it seemed from my school-yard discussions with my classmates. My father had an unhealthy obsession with Martin Luther, the great reformer, as has been made abundantly clear by my name, Luther Anne Martin. No, I do not know what would possess him to think this name would cause me to have any positive emotion toward the Reformer, nor why my mother would allow him to do such violence to his son's future.

He would play games of a sort as well. For instance, we could not eat until we recited the 95 Theses. Once those were memorized, we began the work of looking at Luther's answers for those 95 historic questions. My father quizzed me on history, he drilled me on Luther's biography, he pressed me to learn German and then Greek and Latin and eventually even a smattering of Hebrew. He compared my translations with Luther's and showed me the ways my translations were inferior—how quickly Luther translated them in comparison and how his were much more accurate and beautiful. God forbid that I suggest this was the result of my lack of fluency in the German language. The lecture that followed, often in German as a lesson for the impertinence of the question, would inevitably flay my eardrums with layer upon layer of praise for the great Luther and rhetorical questions about myself in comparison to him. All of which conspired to give me a skewed picture of the importance of Luther. (I understand now that he was, indeed, a great man, but not a god whose every word was golden, as my father seemed to imply. Luther himself would have been disgusted to see the extent of my father's devotion, and I have no doubt most Lutherans would be disgusted by my father's extremes as well. Luther would not have wished to be compared to a god. On the other hand, he certainly would not have hesitated to claim that his reasoning and theology were superior to the Catholic church and her thinkers and, yes, superior to the second-rate reformers, such as Zwingli, who buzzed around Europe like flies.)

My father's inflexibility, his unpleasable nature, and the

paucity of sincere affection all haunted my youth. But as Gabriel García Márquez wrote, "A man knows when he is growing old because he begins to look like his father." I can look back now, and insights about my father's nature and intention become clear to me. He did not intend to teach me theology at the expense of a relationship with himself, or for that matter, with God, though that is what he did. He did not mean to drive my brother out of the house or out of the church, but that is what he did. He did not mean to take his anger and grief about my brother's prodigal lifestyle and use them to turn the screws on my own theological education, but that is what he did.

The night he discovered my true nature I remember very clearly. I had snuck from the house on a moon-full night and spent the hours reveling. Covered in leaves and mud and blood and still dazed, relaxed and sated, I slipped over the fence and in through my bedroom window. He stood there in his night robe, a flashlight in his hand. As I recall I held a live chicken in my own hand, a little snack for home. He looked at me with enviable calm, and without a sound, without a comment, he turned and walked from the room, a look of indescribable disappointment on his face. He did not mention it in the morning, which would have been, to my way of thinking, superior. Instead he slammed a copy of *Concerning Christian Liberty* on the breakfast table and said, "Good theology domesticates our baser instincts."

From then on he spoke to me respectfully but from a distance, both figurative and literal. Never would he come within arm's reach, and he grew colder, more remote. When I tried to speak to him about my condition, which I did on more than one occasion, I would find him silent, impassive, and disappointed. Often

I would find another tome of unenviable size wedged outside my doorway in the morning.

On top of this pressure came the pressure of being the minister's son. For some inexplicable but common reason, the laity expect that the son of a minister must surely be a creature of divine attributes, and if he is not, the minister is the one to blame. Every perceived slip, every slight to an old woman, every shadow of carnal action was one more strike against my father. Not against me, oddly enough, but against my father. This meant that my father must occasionally say to me, "Don't do this or that thing, because it reflects poorly on me as your father." My entire life reflected on him, it seemed, and when I first learned the story of my poor brother, Marty, standing up in the middle of a service and declaring himself an atheist before walking out the door, never to return, I immediately envied him, understood him, and pitied him for his flamboyant dramatic streak. I made my exit more slowly and carefully and perhaps more painfully. I do not miss the irony that both my father's children walked away from his intended path for us, and the fact that perhaps it was because of his parenting after all.

So. You ask me why I hate my father. I can only say that hate, loathing, disgust, all these words would be too strong to explain my feelings for my father. I have felt those things and moved beyond them to a sincere and placid lack of thought about him. He is not part of my life, and I have no interest in altering that whatsoever. I did not invite him to my wedding, and he has never met his granddaughter. If my nature pains him on the level that he told me every day of my life, then I will let my nature be unknown to him. Let him think I am reformed, let him think I am transformed. Let him think I am dead. It means little to me.

What would I say if I were to see him again? I am uncertain. I hope I would treat him amiably, like any other stranger. I hope that even though his presence would be unwanted, I would treat him politely, as one treats a traveling salesman or a solicitor. If I could not do that, I hope I should at least ignore him. I trust that I would save him the pain of knowing anything about me and my life.

CHAPTER 8

WHAT'S MISSING IN CHURCH?
C H _ _ C H

ALL THESE MONSTERS made me nervous. The following Sunday I stood in the bathroom and looked hard into the mirror. I looked normal to me. I took a deep breath, closed my eyes, and leaned against the bathroom counter. I looked normal. Not average, of course. For instance, I was smarter than most people, regardless of the occasional dumb act I put on, which was all part of the plan for manipulating people around me. Other than that, nothing abnormal. No sharpened teeth. No pelt of fur on my face. No rotting flesh or cat eyes or extra appendages. Normal.

I ran down the stairs. "I'm on my way to church with Luther," I told Krista. I had filled her in on my adventure at

Luther's house, and she had listened with the calm but faintly skeptical air of someone who lived with me and was used to the strange events in which I often found myself involved.

Krista crossed her arms over her pregnant belly. "What are you two up to?"

"Just helping him find a church," I said. "I'll be home later."

"How much later?"

I threw up my hands. "I don't know. I'm trying to cure a werewolf here."

"I'm not saying it's not important, I just want to know when you'll be home with me and the kids."

I put my arms around her. "Look, I'm sorry. I know I'm not around as much as I should be. But I need to take care of this. I need to make the world safe for that little baby on the way." I looked in her eyes and saw that grudging look of mild, wavering permission. I smiled, gave her a quick kiss, and slipped out the door.

Luther sat outside in his Lincoln Town Car, "A Mighty Fortress Is Our God" blaring from the open windows. He was taking the whole going-to-church bit pretty seriously. Maybe he was giving it a chance. I climbed in, and we headed off to the First Regular Christian Church of Vancouver. Luther told me it was a medium-sized congregation with a reputation for non-scandalous members who lived lives of admirable decency, and that they occasionally sent postcards in the mail or came by and papered our neighborhood with flyers inviting us to their services.

As we walked in we overheard two young men in their twenties arguing over a theological point. Luther and I slipped to the side of the entrance so we could observe them further. "Watch them," he said. "Listen to this."

"I'm saying that Lordship Salvation is the only way that you can read this verse," said the first man.

"And I'm saying that you are unnecessarily weakening the reality of Eternal Security," said the second man.

"They seem smart," I said to Luther. He nodded. This was a good sign, to my way of thinking. The argument continued at some length.

Finally the second man held up his hand. "Listen, I have a way to settle this once and for all. I have my *Dr. Bokor Study Bible* right here. Let's look up our question in the book, read the commentary, and then we'll know what's right once and for all." A faint bell rang in the back of my mind. I had heard that name somewhere. Dr. Bokor.

To my astonishment the first gentleman agreed to use the study Bible to solve their disagreement, and they opened to the verse in question and read it together. The *Dr. Bokor Study Bible* was, perhaps, the largest Bible I had ever seen. It took two hands to lift and open it, and it was easily the size of a phone book. "Oh," said the first man. "I guess that settles it."

"It certainly does," said the second man.

"That was strange," I said. Luther grinned and led me into the chapel, where we took our seats in a pew covered in what appeared to be orange carpet.

"They seemed to be having a good argument, but as soon as they read that commentary in their Bible they were in complete agreement."

A lady behind us leaned over and tapped me on the shoulder. "It was probably Dr. Bokor's study Bible!" she said, beaming. "He's such a gifted expositor of God's Word! I know that when I have a question about what the Bible means, I always turn to Dr. Bokor."

"Fascinating," Luther said. "And you always agree with this Dr. Bokor?"

"Of course," the lady said, and the man beside her smiled and nodded.

"We all do," said the man. "We're doing our best to follow the Lord, and Dr. Bokor's insights really move us along that path. Why, we started a Bokor seminary here at the church, and we're using his Bible study materials in our Sunday school classes."

"We should give these boys a Bokor Bible, Stan," said the lady.

"We certainly should," said Stan, but just then the music started. I didn't recognize the songs, but about halfway through, Luther elbowed me.

"Look at the copyright information," Luther whispered. So I did. Lyrics by Henry Bokor—on every song. What was going on here?

Soon Dr. Bokor himself took the stage. He was a thin man with a shock of unruly black hair. "Some people," he said, "will tell you that you can't experience real change in your lives. That you must remain a sinful, broken monster of a human being. But that is not so. It's possible—nay, expected—that you be changed. And this can be accomplished through hard work, discipline, and an unwavering commitment to the truth in this book." He held up a *Dr. Bokor Study Bible* with both hands.

I looked around the room. Every person other than me and Luther was dutifully writing down notes. Stan leaned forward when he saw me looking around. "I know you two are looking for answers. I used to be an angry man, but Dr. Bokor helped me."

"I've tried to change," Luther whispered back. "I've tried discipline and hard work, but it doesn't seem to help."

"It's possible," Stan said, "nay, expected—that you be changed. And this can be accomplished through hard work, discipline, and an unwavering commitment to the truth in this book." He tapped the cover of the Bokor study Bible next to him on the pew.

Luther and I turned slowly back toward the pulpit. "Something is weird here," I said. I looked around at the faces of the people in the pews. In a moment of strange insight I realized that their faces were all the precise same color. It was the color of makeup. Pretty close to Bokor's skin color, I noticed. Even the men appeared to be wearing makeup. A cold dread settled on my chest. "This place is creepy. Let's just leave."

"These are good Christians," Luther hissed. "Do you see how they're all wearing the same clothes?" I looked around,

NIGHT OF THE LIVING DEAD CHRISTIAN

and he was right. The women had on floral print dresses, and the men all wore slacks, a blue shirt, and a tie. The ties were different colors, though. Luther held out a pair of sunglasses. "Put these on," he said. "I want to show you something."

"No," I said, my jaw clenched. But Luther pressed them into my palm. I nervously moved them back and forth between my hands.

Stan's wife leaned forward and whispered, "Dr. Bokor says that wearing sunglasses is evil because the Lord said that he who has the Son has life, and we shouldn't want to block out the sun, which is so much like Jesus." I could sense Stan nodding. I looked sideways at Luther, who frantically motioned for me to put the glasses on. I smelled a really unpleasant odor coming from the pew behind us and had a sudden hysterical association between the stink and the word *pew* and had to choke down a laugh. I looked back at Stan, and when he smiled at me again I noticed that he had only a few teeth and that his gums were a dark, rotten green.

My stomach lurched, and to try to hide my nausea I slapped the sunglasses onto my face. Dr. Bokor noticed me from across the room. His face twisted into a frown, and he made a swiping motion. The congregation all reached up and clawed at their own faces, and in a sudden moment of horror I saw the congregation for what they really were. Sticking out from their suits and floral dresses were limbs and heads of rotten, stench-ridden corpses. Mrs. Stan grinned at me, and her mouth too was only half full of teeth, surrounded with greenish flesh.

"Great shades of Elvis," I whispered. And then I shouted, "RUN, LUTHER, RUN! THEY'RE ZOMBIES!"

Dr. Bokor's voice rang out across the auditorium. "Get them, my children. Make them like one of you!" And as if by hidden signals the whole congregation stood and turned toward us. Luther had time to knock down one undead churchgoer before they swarmed us.

CHAPTER 9

BRAINS, BRAINS,
WE WANT YOUR BRAINS

WHEN SWARMED BY ZOMBIES, it is important to stay calm.
This is a lesson we learned because the first thing we did
when swarmed by zombies was to panic. In fact, the first and
only thing I did in this crisis was to wrap my arms around
Luther's neck and jump up into his arms while shouting,
"SAVE ME, WOLFMAN, SAVE ME!"

I felt cold hands closing in on my arms and neck and
strange, dead voices saying, "Do you agree with us or not?"

I looked out over the sea of zombie faces, and in the back
of the auditorium I saw the Hibbs 3000 and Dr. Culbetron.
Dr. C was wearing his lab coat, and Hibbs looked like
an ordinary person as always. "BRAINS!" I shouted, and
pointed at them. I know, that probably seems wrong to you,

NIGHT OF THE LIVING DEAD CHRISTIAN

but you have to admit that keeping your own brains is a powerful reason to sell out your friends. And Culbetron and Hibbs both had such big, juicy brains. Culbetron looked at me sourly, swept up what appeared to be a specimen box, and quickly moved out of the auditorium. "He's getting away!" Luther shouted, and the zombies immediately turned away from us and headed for our friends.

In the momentary zombie clearing, Luther ran with all his might out of the auditorium and through the glass doors toward the exit. But just at that moment Stan lumbered into our path, his dead face twisting into a rictus of a smile. "Where you going?" he asked, and I screamed.

"It speaks!" I said.

"You are not being helpful," Luther said, shoving Stan out of our path. The exit was blocked, so Luther quickly assessed possible escape routes and pushed through a swinging door into a stairwell. We had to make the choice of whether to go up or down. Luther dropped me to the ground and pried my arms from around his neck. "Up or down?" he asked.

"Up," I said confidently. "They'll expect us to run downstairs." I don't know why I said this. I just wanted to sound like I knew what I was talking about. So we ran upstairs as fast as we could, only to hear the moans of the zombified congregation hot on our heels.

"We have to find a door we can bar," Luther said. Three doors were on the outside section of the hallway. (Luther pointed out that this was our best bet for finding a window.) The first door was locked.

"They're getting closer!" We tried the second door, also locked, just as an army of well-dressed undead monsters stepped into the hallway.

"You need to see what our pastor says about going to church," the first zombie said.

"We don't want to!" I shouted.

Luther shook me violently. "Stop talking to them and try to open that third door!"

I raced to the third door and tugged on the handle, but it didn't budge. "Why shouldn't I talk to them?" I asked, so panicked that I scarcely knew what I was saying. Luther shoved a zombie backwards, knocking several of them down, but they kept swarming toward us, shouting incomprehensible phrases and Bible verses and chanting the name of Dr. Bokor.

Luther came up next to me and gave the door a shove. It swung wide open. I had been pulling instead of pushing. He kicked me through the doorway. "For one thing, I think they might be smarter than you," he said. He pushed the door shut, but the zombies already had their hands reaching through the crack. "Help me," he said, and I jumped next to him, slamming into the door with my shoulder. It crashed against the zombies' hands, and with animal squeals they pulled their hands back through as the door bounced back toward us. Luther let loose with a triumphant shout and slammed the door shut.

Except that it didn't shut. I stuck my head around the corner to see that one of the zombies had shoved a copy of the *Dr. Bokor Study Bible* in the gap, and now green, decayed hands were forcing their way through again. With a swift tap I sent the book careening back into the hallway and the door slammed shut at last, but not before one of the zombies looked me in the eye and said, "I have a podcast you should listen to!"

Luther slumped against the door and quickly worked the lock. The door started shivering in the frame almost immediately, and a chant of "Brains! Brains! We want your brains!" started up. We took a quick survey of the room we were in. It appeared to be the pastor's office. It was severe, neat, and carefully maintained. I took a look at the bookshelf. Every book on the shelf had been written by Dr. Bokor, on every imaginable topic. *Predestination: He Chose Me Because My Righteousness Was Filthy Rags (But Less Filthy than a Heathen's)* was the first title I saw, followed by *Achieve Holiness in One Simple Step* and *Poor, Misguided Charismatics*. There were easily thirty other titles, including, of course, the *Dr. Bokor Study Bible*.

Luther threw back the window shade to reveal one giant pane of plate glass with no way to open it. The chanting outside was getting to be annoying, and I found myself muttering, "Brains, Brains, We Want Your Brains," under my breath. Finally I couldn't take it anymore, and I pounded on the door and shouted, "Change it up for a minute, why don't ya? Don't you know any other chants?"

There was a pause, and then one of the zombies shouted, "What do we want?"

And they all answered him, "Your brains!"

"When do we want them?"

"Right now!"

And then the chanting started again, so loud that I almost didn't hear the most terrifying sound of all: a key in the lock of the door. I yelled to Luther, and he spun around in time to watch, as I did, the slow movement of the lock turning toward its opening, and then the door swinging open to reveal a grinning Dr. Bokor, flanked by his zombies.

"Hello, boys," he said. "You should have suspected I would have a key to my own office."

SINGING, JUST SINGING 'BOUT YOUR BRAINS

DR. BOKOR STRODE INTO his office, his face split in a wide grin. His zombies shambled in behind him. He sat in his office chair and watched us happily. "Your two friends escaped," he said nonchalantly. "They surprised us by running downstairs instead of up when they got to the stairwell."

Luther gave me an impolite look. I shrugged. "We've never even met those guys."

Now Dr. Bokor shrugged. "Then you won't mind that I've dispatched some of my parishioners to bring them home and to a, shall we say, right way of thinking." He studied Luther carefully. "Werewolf, are you?"

"As a matter of fact, I do struggle with lycanthropy, not that it's any business of yours."

Dr. Bokor reached to a shelf behind him, removed a book, and threw it to Luther. "You'll find this instructive, I think," he said. I could see the title: *Overcoming Lycanthropy through Careful Theological Reasoning.*

"I suspect that your solution is merely to exchange my lycanthropic state for that of one of your undead thralls," Luther said.

Bokor laughed. "Undead? What is that but another way to say resurrected? Yes, they are shambling, unthinking brutes who agree with the slightest theological utterance I make, but the fact is that it makes them happy and keeps them in line and protects them from many varieties of sin that you yourself can't seem to master."

"But they aren't alive," I said.

"And yet, I don't suppose you could say they are dead," said Bokor.

"I suppose not." The zombies stood mindlessly behind him, uttering the occasional "Amen" or "Preach it, Dr. Bokor."

"As for you," he said to me, "it appears that you haven't yet embraced your true nature as a horror film monster."

I laughed. "Just this morning I looked at myself in the mirror, and I am a normal human being. Even if I were a monster, I could handle it. I have plans in place for such things."

Now Bokor laughed, long and lustily. "Lovely, sir. Lovely. And so representative of the hubris of your kind." He snapped his fingers, and several zombies left the room. "It's time for me to give you a better representation of what I offer here, gentlemen. You are suffering from a series of questions about how, for instance, to control your anger. You are Christians and you cannot understand why your life does not change, and you spend inordinate amounts of time trying to figure it out."

"I am not a Christian," Luther said.

He pointed at Luther. "Your anger drives your loved ones away, I suppose." He pointed at me. "And you, no doubt, agreed to help him 'fix himself' by going to church. In which case, you've come to the right place. Observe."

He stood up behind his desk and put on a top hat. He pulled out a cane and spun it around several times. Zombies reentered the room carrying a variety of musical instruments: a guitar, some bongos, a tuba, and an accordion. "One," Dr. Bokor said. "A-one two three four." And the zombie band began to play an upbeat and lively tune.

Bokor kicked his heels out and began to sing in a lovely tenor voice:

> *You suffer from a basic misunderstanding*
> *Of what it is I do.*
> *You think I'm making zombies*
> *And I want to do the same to you!*
> *But you miss my good intentions*
> *Which is to transform you each today*
> *From suffering, no-good sinners*
> *Into mindless servants of My Way!*

A brief musical interlude followed here, with the zombies—seemingly enjoying themselves—playing a fascinating blend of polka and 1980s praise music (with the accordion doubling as synthesizer). A slightly less-rotten young lady zombie joined Bokor near his desk, and their voices blended as they sang this duet:

> Bokor: *Do you ever have to think, my dear?*
> Zombie Lass: *Not a bit, dear sir, never fear!*
> Bokor: *Do pesky questions ever drive you to drink?*
> Zombie Lass: *I just read your books and learn what I should think!*
> Together: *I'm so glad that we agree when we read Bokor's books of theooooologeeeeeeeeeeeee!*

Caught up in the moment, I started to tap my toes a bit. The music was lively and enjoyable. Dr. Bokor winked at me and said, "Here comes the big finish, sir! Sing along if you like!" He leapt up onto his desk, and the music swelled.

> *It's not me who wants your brain*
> *So you'll never think again,*
> *Never wrestle with moral choices*
> *Or regret your raisèd voices!*
> *Oh, there's only one thing that*
> *will please us—*

(Here all the zombies joined in an impressive multipart harmony.)

> *And that's to give your brain to Jeeeeezuuuuuuus!*

Bokor leaned toward me and sang, "Oh, with sin you won't be messin'," and then he raised his eyebrows at me.

I grinned and sang, "If you never have a question!"

"Right! So it would be smart to give Jesus that special part!"

I sang, "'Cause Jesus wants my brain, not my heart!"

And that, I think, is right about the moment that Luther grabbed me and threw me through the plate glass window.

CHAPTER 11

NO BODY KNOWS
THE TROUBLE I'VE SEEN

WHAT POSSESSED LUTHER to throw me through the plate glass window was a topic of much future conversation. He claimed that he was afraid I was on my way to joining the Undead Band. He also claimed that it was my singing and that his superior, wolflike ears couldn't stand the off-key harmonies. One last thing he claimed was that he needed to break the window somehow, and my head was the largest, hardest item in the room. This I cannot deny, though I did point out that one of Dr. Bokor's study Bibles would probably have been sufficient for the task.

Regardless, I flew through the air much like a brick and also landed much like a brick on the pavement below. Luther jumped down and landed lightly on his feet. I tried to express my displeasure at being thrown out the window, but all I could manage was a weakly sung, "Jesus wants my brain, not my heart." Luther grunted, grabbed me by the belt, slung me over his shoulder, and made for the parking lot.

"I can walk," I said. Luther set me down just as a gaggle of zombies burst out of the church shouting about brains, podcasts, radio shows, and study Bibles.

"Quick!" Luther said, and we ran for his car. But when we got there he couldn't find his keys. He moved his hands frantically through his pockets. The zombies were halfway to us, and I could see the keys on the pavement. Luther must have dropped them. "Get on the passenger side!" I shouted and ran toward the zombies, slid on the ground to the keys, kicked off the corpse-y hands that grabbed at me, and scrambled back to the car, unlocking the door of the Town Car and sliding behind the steering wheel before unlocking the passenger side.

I locked the doors, but not before the zombies completely surrounded us. I started the engine. "Come back next week," one of the zombies said, and another shouted, "Thank you for filling out your friendship card. Now we know where you live."

Luther scowled. "Did you fill out a friendship card, you moron?"

"I didn't know it was a church full of zombies at the time! You might warn a guy about things like that!"

"Drive," Luther said, and I shifted into gear. But as I

popped the car into drive, I noticed a man walking to his car in the far distant corner of the parking lot. Or rather, limping toward it. His flesh looked unhealthy, but not decayed. He dropped his Bokor study Bible, looked at it for a moment, then left it on the ground and limped on again.

"He's not dead yet," I said.

Luther pounded the dashboard. "*We're* not dead yet! Drive, Mikalatos!"

"Look at him." I pointed toward the distance. "Bokor's been turning him into a zombie, but he's not dead yet." I moved the gearshift into reverse. "We have to save him."

"NO! Save us first!"

But I knew, somehow, that I was meant to save that guy. I hit the gas and scattered the zombies like ninepins. A couple of them held on to the hood and started crawling toward the windshield. I slammed it into drive and pushed my foot to the floor. With an enormous squealing of tires and zombies, we lurched into V-8 powered speed. A zombie fell off the car, and I cackled with delight. Luther's hands flew to the safety handle above the window, and he let out a bark of fear.

I laughed again and swerved the car, trying to dislodge the last zombies. We were going to save that half-dead zombie after all! Or at least, that's what I thought. Right up until the precise moment that I hit him with the car.

He flew up into the air, bounced off his own car, and slumped to the pavement. Luther shook his head, swung his door open, and ran over to him. He scooped him up and yelled for me to pop the trunk.

"Just put him in the backseat," I said.

"You unspeakable idiot. You're going to put a zombie in the backseat of the car with us?"

I conceded his point but couldn't find the button to pop the trunk. I jumped out and hurried back to the trunk, getting there at about the same time as Luther. Together we settled the man into the trunk and then closed it. Luther snatched the keys from me. I protested for a moment and then headed for the passenger door. I didn't see a stray zombie climbing out from the car's undercarriage until he had his teeth pretty deeply into my thigh. "OW! BAD ZOMBIE!" I punched at him, then got into the car and locked my door.

Luther peeled out of the parking lot, headed for home. He looked over at my torn jeans. "If you turn into a zombie in my car, I will kill you."

"That's an unpleasant figure of speech," I said.

"I mean it literally."

"You wouldn't do that."

"I threw you through a window a minute ago because I thought you would probably break the glass with your head."

I considered this. "A good point. I will do my best not to turn into a zombie." Luther spent much of the ride home staring at my leg and giving me threatening looks.

A WEREWOLF'S THOUGHTS ON TRANSFORMATION

Thomas Jefferson wrote, "We are afraid of the known and afraid of the unknown. That is our daily life and in that there is no hope, and therefore every form of philosophy, every form of theological concept, is merely an escape from the actual reality of what is. All outward forms of change brought about by wars, revolutions, reformations, laws and ideologies have failed completely to change the basic nature of man and therefore of society."

Here was a man who believed in revolution and the need to transform government, who fought for it, who sacrificed for it. Yet his candid admission at the end of such efforts was that it did not work—could not, in fact, work, because government and revolution and books and laws and a hundred thousand other man-made tools cannot change the basic nature of a human being. Thus we remain as we are. And thus the world remains as it is.

Many Christians I know have unwisely emphasized the eschatological and postmortem benefits of being "born again." They tell me that I will live an interminable and unending life of passable pleasure in some heavenly kingdom best suited to the Middle Ages on gaudy streets of gold and a giant pearl for the front door of my own personal mansion.

Leaving aside the fact that, in comparison to most people in human history, I already live like a king with my large house, my ability to travel enormous distances in a short amount of time, and food that is both plentiful and prepared for me literally around the world, the description of the Christian afterlife is remarkably dull. And the fact remains that I have no intention of living a Spartan life today in the hopes of Elysian fields tomorrow, particularly in the absence of hard data showing what I am buying and at what cost.

Frankly, I want payment now. I want to know that my life will be better today. Christians promise a life of passing pleasantries, and even, depending on their theological convictions and whether or not they appear on television, a life full of the enjoyment of the best and largest house and a lovely wife and expensive car and gold and pearls and a retirement fund. Nevertheless, the Christians with the most conviction seem to accept these things with something bordering on embarrassment if they have them, and to view their absence as an inconvenience or even a virtue. Regardless, all of these things are attainable outside of their philosophy and are, indeed, easier to attain in the absence of Christian ethics.

And so we return to my most pressing need, the desire for transformation, the burning passion to have a more manageable and less destructive nature. Of course, the Christians say they can help with that. Or God can. But I look at their lives and see far too many zombies. That is to say, they claim to have found a new, invigorating, abundant life, but I see little evidence that it's anything but idle chatter. They cheat on their income tax and cut corners at work and yell at their children. They break their wedding vows on Friday night and tighten their ties and straighten their skirts on Sunday morning. They drive by a homeless man on their way to a social justice rally, or they ignore the raped woman crying on the sidewalk while they hoist their antiabortion signs. They're nice enough, perhaps, but are they truly changed from what they were before? I think not. Not any more than a Hollywood starlet is changed in the hour it takes to coif her hair and slather on her makeup.

I say all this to make one simple point: If that's the abundant life, I do not want it. If that is what it means to be "Christian," then I surely do not want to be called by that name. If being Christian means only a certain doctrinal purity—to believe that this and this and this proposition is true about God—then I do not see the value in it.

If belief gets us into Heaven regardless of behavior, or even despite our actions, then Satan will be in Heaven alongside the pastors and theologians and missionaries and saints. For Satan's theology must surely be as informed as the most learned Christian scholars, for he knows God very well indeed. And the signposts Christ gave for recognizing his "true followers" seemed to have very little—in fact, next to nothing—to do with people's beliefs.

He seemed strongly concerned about people's actions. Christians say, "A true disciple of Jesus believes that he is God and that he died for our sins." But the Christ they claim to follow said that his true disciples take up their crosses and follow him, that they obey his teachings, that they "bear much fruit," that they love one another, that they give up everything, even family, to follow him in the way he demands.

It seems that Jesus' own definition is alien to most Christians, who are satisfied that by signing their name on some creed they are somehow mystically associated with Christ. It is why I can say with Mahatma Gandhi, "I like your Christ. I do not like your Christians."

Perhaps if they were more like Christ I would like them too.

CHAPTER 12

MY PET ZOMBIE

AFTER CONSIDERABLE DEBATE, we decided to keep the zombie in Luther's shed, in his backyard. Dr. Culbetron agreed that this would be a workable solution, and he and the Hibbs 3000 spent a great deal of time whispering in a little private knot and then looking through the peephole we had made to keep an eye on the zombie.

The boys also studied my flesh wound with considerable interest before Hibbs said, "This wound will not result in your eventual zombification."

"You don't know that," Luther said. "You always think you know how everything works, but you're just guessing."

"The robot's right," Culbetron said.

"The *android* is correct," Hibbs said under his breath. "As always."

Culbetron gave him a dour look and continued. "We've done considerable research into Dr. Bokor's zombies, and it does appear that there is a low incidence of werewolves in their congregation. This breed of zombies doesn't reproduce through biting." He poked my leg wound with his finger, and I yowled at him. "There are plenty of different ways a zombie plague can start . . . magic, of course, or through a virus, usually spread through bodily fluids, which is why the zombie bite can be so dangerous. I've heard of zombie plagues that can be spread through *hearing other zombies* or even by seeing their acts of violence. This particular breed appears to infect through philosophy."

"Don't be ridiculous," Luther said.

"It's true," Culbetron said. "You heard about their church. The zombies insist that their victims read certain books, listen to certain podcasts. The main question of a zombie race like this is, 'Do you agree with me?' You may recall that when they captured me the other day, they tried to hold me down and force me to listen to a podcast. They can't rest until you've become like them . . . and then you'll want others to become like you. And so it spreads."

I shuddered. "It's frightening. I was getting into it a little during the musical number."

"Your kind tends to have a soft spot for musicals, especially if you're offered a solo."

"My kind? That's the second time someone has implied that *I'm* a monster."

My friends—the werewolf, the mad scientist, and the robot—exchanged glances and then smiled at me. "We're just kidding you," Hibbs said, and they all broke into hilarious laughter.

I looked at them warily. I wasn't sure what was going on. But I was quickly distracted by banging and shouts coming from the shed. "Let me out!" said the zombie.

Hibbs looked in through the peephole. "What's your name?" he asked.

"I only talk to the guy who hit me with the car," said the zombie.

I cleared my throat. "You heard him, men. Stand back and let an expert do the interrogation. Watch a pro for once." I leaned close to the peephole and asked confidently, "What's your name?"

"Robert."

I frowned. "Rob Zombie?"

"*Robert.* Don't call me Rob."

"Well, soorrreee, Roberto. I didn't know you were so touchy. My name is Matt."

"A pleasure to know the name of the guy who hit me with his car, Matthew."

"Uh, it's Matt. Only my close family and friends call me Matthew."

"Well, soorrreeee, Mateo, I didn't know you were so

touchy," he said with a snort. A collection of half-smothered giggles came from my friends.

"Also," I said, "slight correction. It was Luther Martin's car that hit you, not mine. Just in case you're thinking of, for instance, suing someone." Luther scowled at me.

"Sue you? No way. I want to thank you. I've been trying to get up the guts to leave that place for months."

Culbetron cackled with inappropriate laughter. We stared at him, and he chortled, "The zombie just said that he was trying to get up the *guts* to leave. Get it? Guts?"

Luther sighed. "You are like a paperweight on our souls, Doctor."

"We should let him out," I said.

"It is as if you do not recall my advice to stop doing stupid things," Hibbs said.

"Culbetron seems to think the zombie can't infect us except through philosophical means. That means we won't be in any more danger talking to him out here than talking to him while he's captive in Luther's shed."

The boys looked questioningly at Luther, who nodded reluctantly. I jumped up and broke the door open. Robert the Zombie smiled and took hold of my hand. "Thank you," he said. "You are so generous. Now tell me how I can stop living this zombie lifestyle."

"Okay," I said. "First I think you need to stop listening to Bokor completely. I mean, some of his theology is actually good, but you seem to be infected with it rather than helped by it."

"I can do that," Robert said. "In fact, I dropped my study Bible in the parking lot right before you hit me with your car."

"Luther's car," I reminded him.

"What Bible do you use?" Robert asked.

"Oh, I have a pocket-size travel Bible."

"Translation?"

"NIV."

"Color?"

"Blue. With a little silver MM on the flap."

"Okay, I'll get one of those."

I stroked my chin and looked at Robert carefully. He looked healthier, but something still wasn't right. To see Robert coming out of his zombie stupor so quickly and easily gave me hope that we could find a cure for Luther. I tried to think of other things that could help Robert and realized that sometimes the most helpful thing is helping someone else. I laid out the whole thing for him: Luther's condition, his wife leaving him, our plan to try to cure him. Robert listened closely.

"And what do you want me to do?" he asked.

"I want you to join us on our mission to destroy all monsters," I said, pleased to be getting in a reference to a Godzilla movie.

"Then that's what I'll do," he said. "When do we start?"

CHAPTER 13

FAMILY MATTERS

"First things first," I said, looking around at my newly commissioned band of monster hunters. I was proud to have a mad scientist, an advanced cybernetic being, a half-zombie, and a spiritually interested werewolf all helping me out. "First we should think of a name for our club!"

"Nonsense," said Culbetron. "First we should get a snack!"

"Okay, fine. Luther, why don't you get us a snack."

"You may recall that my wife left me over a week ago, and I'm afraid I haven't bought sufficient snacks for entertaining, ah, monster hunters."

I smacked my head with my palm. "Fine. Culbetron, you're on food detail."

Culbetron sighed. "I turned my wife into audio waves. Or sent her hurtling through the space-time continuum. Or sent her into a computer fantasyland. Jury is still out on that one." I stared at him in uncomprehending silence until he said, "I've been living on granola bars and fruit juice in her absence."

I looked to Robert, who quickly assured me he was single, we weren't near his house, and if we were, we would have to share a snack-size bag of Bokor brand organic snack (Joseph's Egyptian Plenty Corn Chips). I locked eyes with the Hibbs 3000, who immediately threw up his hands and said, "Android. Sorry."

"Oh, good grief. Everybody pack it up. We're moving to my place, and we'll get snacks there." Getting a motley crew like ours up, moving, and headed in the right direction took more effort than I care to relate, but eventually we were out on the street and headed toward my house, Culbetron and Hibbs a few feet out in front, Luther sulking by my side, and Robert bringing up the rear like some sort of servile packhorse.

As we crossed in front of Lara's house, the Hibbs 3000 paused. "Your neighbor Lara may have information of value to us."

I looked over at her windows, which had the curtains drawn tight. "Why's that, Hibbs?"

"Given her vampiric condition, it seems likely that she would possess insights into the possibility of reversing Luther's lycanthropic state."

I cocked my head at the android. Luther stood staring at Lara's front door. I thought I saw the curtains ripple inside. "She's not a vampire. I've known her since high school. She's been divorced twice and lives alone now, but that's all. She's not a monster."

"I don't like her," Culbetron said. "And she certainly seemed to be a vampire when she stood behind you and hissed at the zombies."

"Hissed at the zombies? Lara?" Just then I noticed that at my house across the street, Krista was walking out to the van with the kids. She waved me over, and I ran over to give her a hug. The kids were pleased to see me, of course, and they proceeded to treat me like a jungle gym. "Where are you three headed?" I patted Krista's belly. "You four, I should say."

The rest of my crew of monster hunters wandered over. "I'm taking the kids to buy Halloween costumes."

"I'm going to be a princess," Zoey said.

"I'm going to be a cute little bunny," Allie said, wrinkling her nose like a rabbit.

I bundled them into my arms. "That's great, kids!"

Allie put her head on my shoulder. "We miss you, Daddy."

"I'm home all the time. Why would you miss me?"

Zoey said, "It doesn't seem like you're home all the time."

"Come on, kids," Krista said, shooing them into the van. The van is much more practical than the Secret Lair. I call it the Cattle Truck. The kids kissed me and clambered in.

Krista got into the van and waved me around to the driver's side, where I was out of earshot from the rest of the gang. She said, "You had a phone message from someone named Clarissa Martin. Luther's wife. She said you should be careful because the werewolf hunter has figured out the werewolf's identity." I looked across at Luther, who was staring sullenly into the distance.

"You know Luther's the werewolf, right?"

She rolled her eyes. "Yes, Matt, I figured that out some time ago. Do you remember me asking you not to kill the neighbor with slingshots and dimes?"

"Oh yeah."

"She also said the werewolf hunter had paid her a visit and made threatening remarks about how he wasn't going to wait for Luther to take his wolf form. He's planning to kill him when he finds him, wolf or not."

"That's not good." I crossed my arms and thought about it. "I'm not sure what to do."

"Be careful," she said. "That's what you should do."

I drummed my fingers on the hood of the Cattle Truck. The kids were getting restless, and Krista looked uncomfortable behind the wheel.

I gave Krista a quick kiss and told her I'd be careful. She and the kids drove away, just like Luther's family had driven away. But I knew that mine was coming back. Luther had no idea whether he'd see his again or not. I told Luther his wife had called and warned me away from him. He snapped his teeth together and his face went red. "She's doing this to get under my skin." He shook his head.

"Oh. And I should mention that apparently the psychotic monster killer knows who you are now."

Luther sighed. "A psychopath is attempting to murder me, and my only friends are three men whose declared purpose in befriending me was to capture or kill me."

I scratched my chin. "Or cure you. Don't forget, that's our current favorite option. I wonder, though, do you think it would be helpful to talk to someone who has been there and been through all this? Because it turns out that I may be friends with a vampire."

Luther grinned. "I suppose it would be worth a try."

"Boys," I said. "Turn around and cross the street. We're off for an interview with a vampire."

CHAPTER 14

FACE OF THE VAMPIRE!

As we rang Lara's doorbell, I wondered briefly why it was that I kept ringing the doorbells of monsters in my neighborhood. I thought back to the novel *Dracula* and tried to remember whether Van Helsing went up to Dracula's castle and rang the doorbell. It seemed likely in Victorian times of polite interaction that everyone probably started out with civil conversation before any biting or staking or violence. But this was the twenty-first century. I should probably bash in the monsters' doors with a SWAT team. Oh well. I made a note to myself to do that next time—if I could find a SWAT team for hire.

No doubt you are thinking I am an idiot not to realize

that my old high school friend was, in fact, a vampire. In my defense, it happened after high school, and also I can be pretty unobservant. Yes, that's right. That's my defense. In any case, I knocked on the door and rang the doorbell and waited for a while. Since it was daylight I wondered for a minute if she could even answer the door, but she did answer it. She swung the door open, and her hair was up in a towel and she had a green facial mask plastered all over her face. She wore a beat-up T-shirt with *American Gothic* on it, and fuzzy pink sweats that hung loosely all the way down to her bunny slippers, which peeked out from beneath her robe with cute little black eyes and floppy white ears. I had expected something a little more terrifying and glamorous.

"Hi, Matt," she said. "What's up?" She glanced briefly at the collection of neighbors and friends around me on the porch, and one eyebrow arched up. "Selling candy or something?"

"Something like that. It actually has more to do with, you know, monsters."

She leaned against the doorway, arms crossed. "Monsters? I don't understand. Is that why your friend there is dressed up like a zombie?"

Robert moaned and put his hands over his face.

"That's the thing, Lara. He sort of is a zombie. Or a half-zombie. I'm not sure how that works. And our neighbor Luther here is a werewolf, and well, we were sort of hoping you might have some advice."

"I don't know why I would have any advice about being a werewolf. Stay away from silver bullets, I guess."

Luther stepped forward, his hands thrust into his pockets, his eyes cast down toward the step. "Please, miss. I know it is probably painful to discuss your condition. But my marriage is at stake, and possibly my life."

Culbetron snickered. "He just said 'at stake' to a vampire. Hee hee hee."

Luther rolled his eyes. "Good night, man, compose yourself." He turned his attention back to Lara. "There is a werewolf hunter following me, and my hope is that if I can reverse the lycanthropic effects, he will release me. Otherwise his intention is to murder me. His name is Borut."

Lara's eyes widened, and she quickly looked up and down the street. "Borut?" She threw the door open wider. "Come in, quickly."

We jostled one another and crowded into her house, and she ordered us to walk straight down the hallway and into the living room. I lingered by the door, and she shut it tight and lifted a heavy bar and set it across the door. "Wow, Lara, I had no idea you were so worried about thieves."

"Not thieves. Borut. I *thought* he was in the neighborhood again." She swept past me into the curtain-darkened living room, where she quickly took an assessment of my friends. "You," she said, pointing at Robert, "take the back door. You'll find a small sliding panel at about eye level. You, the tall one in the lab coat and the taller one with the mechanical walk, you two go upstairs and find a window."

Robert said, "But what are we looking for?"

"A short man with a broken face, carrying about ten times

as many weapons as you would expect. Crossbows, guns, stakes, knives, steak knives, sporks, grenades, water guns full of holy water. He'll have it all."

The three of them got up and did as she said. Lara could be pretty commanding, even in her sweats. Like a PE teacher. She settled into an easy chair and motioned to the love seat across from her. Luther and I sat down at the same time and got wedged in. He tried to scoot away and I tried to stand up, but it was no good. We were not going to be able to share the seat without touching. We tried rearranging, but it wasn't working, so I crossed my legs and leaned away from him and pretended we weren't touching. I quickly introduced the werewolf to the vampire and wondered if this had been a bad idea. My pop culture knowledge assured me that when a werewolf and a vampire meet they either fight each other for dominance or they team up to kill humans. Or in rare cases, they form a World War II squad of monsters and fight Nazis. That would be my favorite outcome, actually.

Lara leaned back and looked up at a mirror above her fireplace. "How long have you been a werewolf, Luther?"

"My entire life, I suspect. Although my first clear memories of it come from when I was a teen. My father always pushed me on it and tried to teach me to control it. He was not . . . forgiving . . . with my lapses."

She tapped her fingers on the arm of her chair. "Borut will leave you alone if he learns that you've managed to overcome your monstrous nature. I used to be a vampire, as apparently someone has mentioned to you. But once I was cured he left me alone. Or mostly alone. He still comes sniffing around every once in a while."

Luther's body went rigid beside me, and the hairs on the back of my neck stood on end. I leaned forward, or tried to. I was wedged in pretty tight. "Wait. You're saying vampirism can be cured?"

She waved a hand dismissively at me. "Of course it can. Vampires, werewolves, zombies, mummies—they can all be cured." She studied Luther carefully. "If they want it badly enough."

CHAPTER 15

THE CURE

Luther looked like he was about to jump out of his skin. I didn't blame him, given Lara's pronouncement that she could provide the answer to all his problems: a cure to his lycanthropy. He said, "Without reservation, madam, I assure you that I am deeply interested and would be most grateful for your assistance."

"I could introduce you to the man who taught me the cure, if you like."

I couldn't believe they were so calm about it. "Lara, how does it work? What's the secret?"

She smiled, and despite her green face and her hair piled on top of her head in a towel, I was reminded of how beautiful she was in high school, and how tired her eyes looked now. I was moved by a sudden old affection, and I wondered what her life had been like as a vampire, and how that had happened. But the more important question, the question of the cure, loomed larger in my mind. "I think it would be better if I started by telling you a little about my story." She held up a hand. "Don't worry, I'll get to the cure. But you need to know the context of how it all happened. I became a vampire just after high school. Matt, do you remember my boyfriend, Jake?"

I knew Lara well enough to realize that she wouldn't budge once she made up her mind. And I was interested in her story anyway. "Sure. I never liked him much. Your first husband, right?"

"Yes. I liked him, of course. He was so charming, and he would take me to the most wonderful places. He was polite and funny and generous. He could be odd, but they were such silly little things . . . how he hated to look at himself, and the way that he insisted our dates always be at night, and how he wore sunglasses even in his apartment during the day. I wanted to wait until we were married to make love, and he agreed to that readily enough, though I'll admit there were plenty of nights when we debated that while half clothed.

"One night he was so frustrated and angry about the whole thing that he stormed out of my apartment and left me for several hours. He came back after he had calmed down, but as I ran my hand over his jacket I felt something sticky and warm. When I pulled my hand away, my fingers were covered in blood. He tried to laugh it off, but I wouldn't drop it and he started to get angry. He kept telling me that I didn't really know him, not really, and I said I wanted to spend the rest of my life with him but I had no idea how short that life might be . . . or how long.

"He started yelling at me then, and I tried to get away from him. I had never seen him like this before. He started saying he was going to teach me a lesson I would never forget, and I was yelling at him to get out of my apartment. When it was clear he wasn't leaving, I grabbed my car keys and I tried to get past him to the door, but he hit me in the stomach and I fell on the floor. I had never felt anything so painful before. Not just the punch to the stomach—I thought I was going to throw up, and my head was pounding—but that he would do that to me.

"I thought he loved me, but now I realize that he was not thinking of me at all, that he loved me because I took care of him, and that when he thought I didn't understand, then I was nothing to him. Less than nothing. He was trying to punish me so I would stay with him and do what he said. I didn't know all that at the time. I've figured it out in the years since."

Luther had a sick look on his face, and he wasn't looking at Lara anymore. I couldn't even tell if he was listening. He seemed to be deep in thought. I knew Lara's first husband had been abusive. She didn't tell me, exactly, but she had written this short story about a woman whose husband saw her driving without her seat belt and rammed his car into hers to get her to pull over and shouted at her to take her safety seriously. It went on from there to pretty disturbing places. I told her that it was a chilling portrait of an abusive relationship, and she looked at me in surprise and said, "I was just writing out one of the fights that Jake and I had last week." She didn't seem aware of what it all meant, and how far down a path of insecurity and fear he had taken her already.

Luther sighed with a sound like the whole world was on his shoulders, like the air in his lungs was too heavy to pump in and out. "I am sure your husband regretted his actions. I am sure if there were some way he could take it all back, he would do so."

"He wasn't my husband yet. And, yes, Luther, that is nearly word for word what he said. It's what abusers often say." The color drained from Luther's face. "But he wasn't done yet. He grabbed me by the arms, and when I kicked and struggled and screamed it only seemed to make him angrier. Or more excited, I'm not sure which. His grip was so tight I had bruises later. He pinned me down, and he bit me, hard. I could feel my skin tearing. I was sobbing, and he pulled his face up long enough to tell me to shut up, that I had asked for this, that I had wanted to know where he had been and what he had been doing and now I was going to know. His face was covered in blood, and I was feeling light-headed and I was so scared."

She stopped, and there was silence for a long time. Luther said nothing. He had found a spot on the carpet that interested him, and he stared at it with unfocused eyes. Lara had never told me any of this, and I found myself wishing she had. How many years had she had carried this alone?

"Afterward, he brought me a warm washcloth, and he cleaned me up and bandaged my neck. He rubbed my back and told me he loved me and would never hurt me and he was so sorry." Her hand went to her neck. Her palm cupped over it, and she stroked it softly. "I believed him, of course. I wore a turtleneck to work after that. It took a long time to heal."

"And that's how you became a vampire? I'm so sorry, Lara."

She looked up at me and smiled with the sort of smile that makes you realize that someone knows a great deal more than you do, and that they see you as a child because you just don't understand. "Matt. Being bitten once doesn't make you a vampire. A few things have to happen. For most people, you have to be bitten several times. For me . . . it was at least seven times that happened, that Jake did that to me. Before we were married." She gripped the arms of her chair and flexed her jaw. "The second thing is that you have to bite someone else."

My stomach dropped. "You did that to someone else?"

She nodded. "Yes. I don't like to talk about it." She stood up and looked at herself in the mirror that hung over her fireplace. "That was the day I stopped looking in the mirror, Matt." She pulled off her towel and grabbed a brush from nearby and started to brush out her hair.

"I was so ashamed. I considered leaving Jake, but he told

me no one would ever want me now. That I was damaged. That I was no good, that I was lucky to get someone as good as him. And I believed him. He kept hurting me. In fact, now that I was a vampire he didn't have to be so careful with me. I wasn't so fragile as before."

"I would never do that to my wife," Luther said. "I would never harm her on that level. I would never make her into what I am."

I debated whether to say something. Luther said he wanted to be free, but at what cost? Would he listen to the truth? I wasn't sure. I said it anyway. "She's only safe because she left you, Luther. How long would she have had to stay in that house before her story would be the same as Lara's?"

He growled at me, and his hands curled up as claws began to sharpen and pierce from his fingers. Lara smacked him, hard, across the face. "Not in my home," she said sternly. Luther, with a strange look of resignation, turned his face back toward the carpet.

Lara gave him a hard stare, but then her face softened and she continued. "My story doesn't change much from there. I lived the life of a vampire. It spiraled downward, slowly at first. I started being unable to deal with sunlight and eventually had to leave my job, which was a relief in some ways. Around this time is when Borut started showing up, stalking us at night when we went out to hunt.

"Jake's anger started focusing somewhere else. I knew he was with other women now, and often. I found him once at our home with one of them, and he looked up at me and smiled and said hello. There was nothing I could do about it, but I started to see that I needed a way out. I moved out of his bedroom and into my own, and he didn't seem to care. He barely acknowledged me any longer, and soon I felt more like a ghost than a vampire. One night after he came home with his arms full from a successful hunt, and I was home and we were ready to sleep, I left the front door unbolted and went to my room."

I held up my hands. "I don't get it. You left the door unbolted?"

"So Borut could get in. I wanted it to be over. He did come in, but he woke Jake, and they had a bloody fight in the house. I went to Jake's room, and I found a woman there, covered in blood. I quickly wrapped a sheet around her and gave her the keys to my car, and she stumbled out of the house.

"When I found Borut and Jake, they were in the kitchen. Borut's left arm was hanging limp, and Jake was cornered near the oven. When I came in, Borut shouted at me to stand back and held a crucifix in my direction. The pain from that crucifix . . . I had been avoiding mirrors, but this was a thousand times worse. It was like someone had turned on some internal heater in my blood, and it was starting to boil. I fell to my knees.

"Jake screamed and leapt for Borut—I'd like to think in an effort to protect me, but I don't know that—and Borut turned and drove a stake into his heart. Jake fell to the ground, and Borut pounded it in with a mallet. Jake looked at me, and his last words were, 'This is your fault.' Then he was gone."

I scratched my head. "I always thought Jake left you."

She barked a laugh completely absent of humor or mirth. "He did. I vacuumed up his ashes later that night. I crawled over to Borut and begged him to kill me, but he kept holding that cross over me and chanting something. He leaned close and said, with that thick Eastern European accent, that he would give me three months to 'get clean.' He said that because I had let the girl go, he would let me go. I held onto his legs and kept begging him to kill me, but he wouldn't. Not yet, he said. He shook me off and left me there in my ruined kitchen.

"Not much changed after that. My second husband was a lot like Jake. I just—well, I just felt comfortable with him. I don't know if he knew I was damaged goods, if he sensed it somehow? But he found me easily enough. One night after a long binge I stumbled into the house, flush with blood but feeling empty, and I went into our bathroom and pulled down the sheets we had put over the mirrors. I looked in the mirror, and I looked awful—"

"Wait a minute, I thought that vampires couldn't see themselves in mirrors."

"That's not exactly true. Vampires don't like to see themselves in mirrors because they don't want to see what they are, they don't want to be reminded of it. If you never see yourself the way that you really look, it's pretty easy to be satisfied with your life. But once you look in that mirror . . . it's hard not to hate what you've become."

I sighed. All my hard work watching vampire movies as a kid was coming to an end. Vampires could see themselves in mirrors? Unthinkable. "What's next? You going to tell me that vampires aren't afraid of garlic?"

She laughed. "There was this vampire who really loved garlic who started that rumor back in the 1500s so he wouldn't have to season his own food."

"Stop distracting her," Luther said, still staring at the carpet. "Let her get to the part where she finds her miracle cure."

"Right," she said. "I looked at myself in the mirror and realized I didn't want to be that person anymore. I wanted to die, if that's what it would take to be changed. Borut never showed up at the end of the three months, but I remembered the way that cross had burned when he held it in front of me. So I looked up a church on the internet, and I went there. The pastor there was a monster hunter too, believe it or not. And he showed me how to stop being a vampire by giving my life to Christ Jesus."

Luther snorted. "And you were instantaneously changed? Transformed from darkness into light?"

Lara tapped her fingers against the chair. "Yes and no. Something changed when I spoke to the pastor. Looking in a mirror became easier, but harder, too. I still hunted sometimes, but more and more often that desire seemed to be leaving me. Instead of a vampire who had a few human urges, I felt more and more like a human with a few vampiric urges." Her hand moved nervously to her neck, and she turned her face away from the mirror. "There are still days when I wish for the easy way out. Dead is easier than undead."

There was a clattering from the front door, and an enormous shuddering boom. Robert came running in from the back. "Uh. I think I saw your guy go past."

"What did he look like?" I snapped.

"Short, crushed face. Slavic. Ticked off. Also, he just threw some sort of Molotov cocktail or bomb or something against the door. That's probably the best identifying factor."

Lara jumped up and took hold of Luther's hand. "There's hope for you still, Luther Martin." She pressed a business card into his hand. "If you can beat this thing, Borut will leave you alone. He has to—it's one of the rules."

"We need to get out of here," I said. "He might be after werewolves, but I'm pretty sure silver bullets kill us regular people too."

An enormous blow sent the sound of splintering wood through the house, and I shouted up the stairs for Hibbs and Culbetron. They came running down just as the door gave way, and the little man stood dramatically with smoke and flames billowing around him as he proclaimed, "O willainous verevolf! I vill kill you at last."

CHAPTER 16

DER VEREVOLF UND DER SHRINK

"THE BACK DOOR," Lara hissed, and she stepped between Borut and Luther. "He's not yours, Borut. Not today."

His eyes narrowed, and he settled a rather impressive rifle onto his shoulder. "You I am remembering. The wampyr voman."

I hustled the boys down the hallway toward the back door, but I looked back just in time to see the flash of light from the muzzle of the rifle and Lara flying up against the wall, a splash of blood covering the wall in seemingly the same moment that the report of the rifle hit my ears. I heard the back door opening and someone shouting at me to come, but I was transfixed by the sight of Lara dropping to the floor, and the vampire hunter reloading his rifle while he stepped toward her. He put the rifle to his shoulder again, and I shouted Lara's name. Her eyes popped open, and she looked over at me with a face that communicated stern disapproval.

"It's just bullets, you idiot," she said, and she stood up and snatched the rifle away from Borut, the blood from her chest wound soaking her T-shirt. She bent the rifle barrel and tossed it aside, then grabbed Borut by the shirt and threw him against the far wall. She looked down the hallway and saw me still standing there and said, "What are you waiting for? Take Luther to the church and get him to the man on that card. I'll hold Borut as long as I can."

I stood there for another long moment, shocked by all the blood and the violence. Television had not sufficiently numbed me to the reality of the gore in front of me, and I made a secret vow to watch more violent television and movies so I wouldn't freeze up like this in the future. "You're still a vampire, Lara."

Her face crumpled, and she looked like a little girl for a moment. But the moment passed, and her eyes and mouth set into a stony look of resolve. "When I need to be, Matt. Now go." Borut was dusting himself off, and he held a sharpened stake in one hand and a crucifix in the other.

"I know vhere you liff," he said to me. "And vhen I am done vith the wampyr I vill come to visit you. No one who is friends vith so many monsters can be vithout sin himself." He lunged for Lara, but she turned into a thick mist for an instant, then brought her fist down on his head.

"Run!"

I ran. From Lara's backyard I jumped the fence and came out across the street from my house, where I saw the boys yelling and motioning for me to hurry. I pulled out my car keys, and we all piled into my ancient, wheezing little Toyota Corolla, freshly topped with gas the day before, though it was still missing a back passenger door from our scrape with the zombies. Luther got in the front seat, and Hibbs, Culbetron, and Robert piled into the back with a great deal of arguing and complaining. I slammed the car into reverse, we scraped bottom across the curb, and within minutes we had left my neighborhood behind.

"Should you call your wife and tell her not to let any Eastern European monster hunters into the house?" Culbetron asked.

"Oh, that's a family rule," I said. "She knows better." I reached across and grabbed the creased and torn business card out of Luther's hand. "Let's see where we're headed."

"We're not going there," Luther said. "We need a different plan."

The card said THE SHELTER LUTHERAN CHURCH OF VANCOUVER. And underneath it, in much smaller letters, REVEREND FRANK MARTIN. "What's the problem? I know where this place is."

"The problem is that the church in question is my father's church. And I will not enter that church so long as any other option remains."

"There is a 97 percent chance that Borut will destroy you

if you do not find a solution," Hibbs said impassively. "And a 3 percent chance that some other, less experienced werewolf hunter will do it instead."

"That's not helpful, Hibbs," I said.

Culbetron smiled. "On the contrary, statistics are always helpful. Keep them coming, Hibbs."

Robert leaned forward. "What about a psychologist? Some of them specialize in behavioral modification. What if we found someone who could help you stop acting like a werewolf? Wouldn't that do the trick?"

Luther rubbed his chin. "I'm not certain. But it would be worth an attempt. Matt, where would you suggest I search for a shrink?"

"Me? Why me?"

"You've clearly had psychological issues in your past. I merely assumed you would be able to give me a referral."

"Why not Culbetron? He's the mad scientist."

Culbetron waved his hand. "Eccentric genius."

I sighed and put my head down on the steering wheel. "I hate shrinks. But I guess I could take you to see Dr. van Pelt." I had to start seeing Dr. van Pelt after my first book, *Imaginary Jesus*, came out. With all the hallucinations of Jesus and time travel and talking donkeys, my boss thought it would be wise for me to get some professional help, even though I had explained to him numerous times that those were just literary devices. Nevertheless, he had insisted that I visit Dr. van Pelt. I didn't like her that much.

I turned the car to take a left on Highway 99 and get

us moving toward Dr. van Pelt's office, and Robert leaned forward again and said, "Master, what do you have against psychologists? They can be super-useful in helping people overcome certain issues in their lives."

I looked at him in the rearview mirror. Had he just called me "master"? Or did he say "mister"? And which one would be weirder? "I know, I know, and I've sent plenty of people to see counselors and it has been, by and large, very helpful for them. I have good friends who are counselors and psychologists, and I would completely trust them with other people's brains. But I had an experience as a child with a psychologist that has turned me off to personally embracing it."

Hibbs laughed. "Perhaps a psychologist could help you overcome this."

"Why did you have to go to a psychologist in the first place?"

"None of your business," I said. "But suffice it to say that I never played with matches again after that."

"So it worked," Culbetron pointed out happily.

It's true. It worked. And the real reason I had to go to the school counselor—who I guess might not even have been a psychologist, who knows? I was ten years old, for crying out loud—was not because of matches, but because I was faking sick all the time to get out of school. We had just moved, and for some reason, I would fake sick. I wasn't particularly good at it. I remember seeing in a movie that you could hold a thermometer up to a reading light and get a high temperature on it, so when my mom left the room I held it up. It was an ancient thermometer complete with mercury, and I could never read it correctly, so I couldn't tell if I was getting it hot enough. So when I heard Mom coming I popped it back in my mouth and burnt my tongue. She took it out and looked at it, then gave me a skeptical glare.

"What's it say?" I asked, really hoping it somehow said that I should stay home and read comic books in bed.

"It says you're dead. You have a fever of a hundred and fifteen degrees. Get your clothes on. You're headed to school." And thus, eventually, to the school counselor.

Looking back, maybe it's not counseling I hated so much as my counselor being an idiot. He was, after all, just a man, and I honestly believe that I may have been smarter than him. Our conversations would go something like this.

Dr. Mann: "Draw a tree."

So I would draw a tree. My mom had recently shown me how to draw a tree, so I drew it just how she showed me. I drew long, questing branches going up, and pretty much the same thing for roots going down. I put a hole in the middle of the tree and scribbled circles over the branches. Then I drew a cute little squirrel with big buckteeth, just for kicks.

Then he would say, "This picture shows that you are confused. Notice the swirling lines around the branches. They indicate confusion. And the hole in the tree shows that you are feeling empty inside, and the roots mean that you are looking for something, reaching out for something."

Then I would say, "My mom taught me how to draw that. So I guess what you're saying is that my mom is confused and empty and reaching out for something. The only thing I actually drew myself is the squirrel. What does that say about me?"

He didn't answer. Instead he got a little huffy and told me to draw a family, but not my family. So I saw what his game was and I drew my family, but I added an extra cat. When I handed him the picture, he handed it back and said, "I have a file here that tells me about your family, and I can see that you drew your own family. A mother and father and two sisters. Now try again, and this time draw a family, but not your family."

So I added a baby and I gave him back the paper, and he got a big grin on his face and said, "This is the family you wish you lived in."

"No, I wish to live with my actual family."

"If that were the case you would have drawn your actual family."

"I did. You told me I wasn't allowed to do that. Do *you* wish I lived with some other family? Let's draw a picture of the counseling practice you wish you had."

He crumpled up the paper and glared at me. This time he said to draw a house but not my house, and knowing it wasn't in my file I drew my house anyway. When he said that was the house I wanted to live in, I told him he was absolutely right because I had drawn my own house. Then he told me to draw myself, and I drew myself in a cute little lab coat, with a table of strange, boiling liquids and some jars on a table, and I was happy and smiling and waving out at the viewers, as if I could see them. *Hello, viewers!*

Then he said, "Do you see how small you've drawn your-self? You are unhappy and have low self-esteem." Did he notice the smiling? Did he notice the waving? He did not. And believe me, self-esteem is not something I've been lacking in life.

I wondered out loud if I could draw a picture of myself doing something, but not what I was doing at this exact moment. He seemed to consider that for a moment, and then he said, "Draw a picture of whatever you like. Free draw." Which was like a gift from Heaven, I was so happy, so I drew a big space battle with a giant ape in a space suit batting away some tiny prop planes (with me flying the lead biplane, shaking my fist at him across the airless void), giant space cruisers chasing little bounty-hunter ships, a shoe, a space cat, some flying saucers, a guy in an aloha shirt wearing glasses shaped like stars, and some other stuff like that.

When I handed him the paper he just looked defeated, and he said, "I can't do anything with this. This is meaning-less. This reveals nothing about you." Which was, as you can guess, not true at all. It revealed a great deal about me and was, in fact, the most revealing thing I had drawn that day. It showed me, far from home, fighting as hard as I could in the cold reaches of space against a giant monkey invader, and all around me there were things I loved and moments of humor and also a shoe in space. And comic books. If only I could have drawn girls I would have thrown a couple of those in there.

We did this, or some variation of it, every week for an hour or so. I told him early on that I did not like chocolate, so every week at the end of our session he would offer me a chocolate chip cookie. Every week I would tell him that I didn't like chocolate, and he would say, "All children like chocolate." One week I asked him for popcorn because he had a popcorn machine behind his desk, but he shook his head and said not until I started eating the cookies he provided me. Looking back, I think if he could draw a picture that would describe how he felt it would be a picture of him hating children and possibly popping balloons at a birthday party. I actually spoke to him once years later, and he told me that he preferred people older than thirty. Which would have been nice to know back when he was counseling a school full of ten-year-olds. Not to say that he didn't know more than most people about the power of meta-analysis in the Solomon four-group design or Bayesian interpretation of frequentist procedures for a Bernoulli process—it's just that he didn't like kids, and he didn't do much to help me overcome my behavior pattern of faking sick. Except in the sense that when I went to my mom and tried to explain that this guy was a complete nut job who I hated and never wanted to see again, she shrewdly struck a deal by saying, "If you never skip school again, you never have to see the school counselor." Which was a deal I agreed to and kept. Well played, Mom.

None of which had much to do with my feelings of dislike for my current counselor, Dr. van Pelt. She was a harpy. Not a literal harpy—I could see how in a story like this one that might be confusing. She was, to be clear, a figurative harpy. Which is to say, she was crabby. All the time. But on the plus side, she was surprisingly inexpensive. Also on the plus side, she didn't have a lot of patients. So when I slammed the car into the parking lot and we all poured out of it and through the glass door into her waiting room, it was like I had brought the mother lode of wackos needing counseling. Most psychologists would have, I'm sure, seen dollar signs, swimming pools, fancy cars, and lives of excess punctuated by sixty-minute sessions of absolute raging torture. Not Dr. van Pelt. She came storming out of her office and demanded to know why I hadn't made an appointment. She had her dark hair up in a bun and that same blue dress that she always wore. It must be her work dress or something.

I leaned against the receptionist desk. "It's sort of an emergency, Doc."

"I told you never to call me Doc. What happened? Did you see the talking donkey again? Did you say what I told you to say?"

I sighed. "I told you, Daisy was a literary device representing the personification of Spirit-infused Scripture in donkey form, and if I did see her I wouldn't say to her what you want me to say, because she would kick me with her donkey legs and that would hurt. No, I brought you a werewolf."

Now it was Doc's turn to sigh. "Another of your ridiculous inventions, no doubt."

"Doc, I'm telling you, he really is—" I had a sudden realization that Dr. van Pelt thought I was crazy. I mean, she *already* thought I was crazy. So giving her a big speech about Luther being a werewolf wasn't going to help. In fact, it might make things worse. So I took another tack. "He is really under the impression that he's a werewolf."

The muscles around Dr. van Pelt's eyes twitched, and her permanent scowl deepened into its more pronounced form. She kept her eyes on me and said, "And is he?"

I laughed nervously and tried not to look her in the eyes. "Pshaw. That's like asking if I'm Bigfoot. Of course not. Ha ha. Yeah, right. And I rode here on the Loch Ness Monster."

"Very well. I'll meet with him. And you, the one dressed like a zombie. I have an open appointment on Wednesday at noon. Be there." She stood up and studied the rest of our crew carefully before pointing her finger at Luther. "You're the so-called werewolf, I take it."

"Correct," he said, with a note of surprise in his voice.

"Come along then. Let's get you fixed up, you poor deluded soul."

CHAPTER 17

WHAT A VAMPIRE HAS AT STAKE

I FOUND LARA ALONE IN her house, fully clothed in a pair of jeans and a pink hooded sweatshirt and sitting among the detritus of her ruined living room. Her dark hair framed a face full of dark looks and reflected, I felt certain, even darker thoughts. She didn't look up when I came in, just poked at the shattered glass and ruined plaster on the ground with a stick. "He got away."

I shrugged. "At least you're okay."

"I'm not okay. I haven't been okay for a long time. And he always, always gets away. He's more a force of nature than a man, I think. Did you get Luther to the church?"

"No, he wanted to go to a psychologist first."

She laughed. "It might help change his behavior, but it won't change what he is."

"What do you mean?"

"You'll see soon enough."

Robert came into the room and said, "Matt, I was hanging around outside waiting for you, and I'm wondering what I should do."

"You could help clean up in here, I guess." Robert grunted and set to work. Culbetron and Hibbs had disappeared again, but I knew Robert would stick around.

Lara actually seemed to show some interest in Robert. "He likes to do whatever you say, doesn't he?"

I scratched the side of my face and considered this. "He's half zombie. I guess he's easily influenced."

Lara stood up, took my arm, and walked me through the trashed house and out the back door onto her porch. We looked down into the small creek that ran down the middle between her row of houses and the houses from the next neighborhood over. She pulled her hood up over her head, and I realized it was because the sun was shining through the clouds.

"You okay?"

She patted my hand with her own, and I noticed for the first time how cold her hands were. "When you pointed out that I'm still a vampire, Matt, that hurt. Not that I didn't know already, I've always known. Reverend Martin showed me how to destroy that part of me, but it's not an easy thing. It's simple, but it's not easy." She picked at the splintered wood on the deck. "Vampires aren't alive and they aren't dead, and it's easier to kill them than bring them back to life. I'm still gasping for air."

I leaned on the rail of the porch and watched the water move down toward the storm drains or wherever it went.

"What did he tell you? Reverend Martin?"

She sighed. "It wasn't just one conversation. We talked for a long time, and you'd be better off hearing it from him. But here's the thing about vampires. We're a mockery of God. We're a purposeful satire of the plan to save humanity from itself. Christians talk about the blood of Jesus being the power of salvation. You know the whole thing, right? God sent his Son to die for us. We're depraved, messed up, twisted creatures."

"Sinful."

"Right. That's the church word. Sinful. We aren't hitting the mark of what God desires us to be. We 'fall short of the glory of God.' So God sent Jesus to die for us, because if you're a vampire or a werewolf or a zombie or whatever, death is what comes for you eventually. But Jesus was sent to take our place, and he died so we wouldn't have to. His blood becomes our chance for life. And that's where the vampires— we take it all and twist it. We say, no, we can live forever ourselves. We don't need God, we don't need the blood of Jesus. We can get it ourselves. We can take little bits of life from the people around us to bolster our own, and whereas the blood of Jesus is freely given, we take it by force from whomever we please. His blood comes from a willing sacrifice, ours comes from our victims." She stopped and looked down at her pale hands. "Once you taste the blood of others, you crave it."

"That's crazy, Lara. You talk like there's an army of vampires out there, like there's millions of people in the world who are feeding off the blood of the people around them. You're the first vampire I've ever met, and I didn't even know you were one until this morning."

Lara put her head in her hands and laughed. "You don't have to suck blood to be a vampire, Matt. It's a question of selfishness, of putting yourself and your needs ahead of the people around you. I'll give you an example. Let's imagine for a minute an industry that's built up around using poor people to provide cheap labor so that the manufacturers can get rich by selling goods to people who are fantastically wealthy. Can you guess which industry I'm referring to?"

"Clothing? Shoes? What are you talking about, sweatshops? I don't know. Cell phones or batteries or something."

"So who is the vampire in that story? The manufacturer? The stores that sell the product? You, the consumer? And what about diamonds? Or agriculture? Or the food industry?"

I shook my head. "You're making things up. There's no way that every industry is a sign of vampirism in the world."

"I'm not saying that. I'm giving you examples so you can understand. How about the man who can do everything himself. He doesn't need help in anything. He takes what he wants, and he's sufficient for any task. He works hard. He is generous with others. He thinks the greatest possible good for the people around him has to do with taking care of himself first.

And he thinks he doesn't need the help of Jesus to be saved, because he can find life-giving sources for himself.

"That man, the one who is so industrious, he tries not to notice how when his girlfriends get to a certain stage in the relationship, when they really start to need him, that this is the time he cuts things off and moves on to the next girl. Because he's not interested in giving, he's interested in getting. If that ratio starts to slip, then it's time to move on. Because vampires don't make sacrifices, they sacrifice others to themselves. And soon we can't look in the mirror anymore, because we hate the idea that the cell phone we're carrying is evidence that we are sucking the life out of some Vietnamese village thousands of miles away. And that man—" she stopped, and her eyes fluttered before she looked at me. "The vampire is always concerned first and foremost about himself. When is the next drink coming? From whom? And how long will the fix last?"

"But I thought Reverend Martin showed you how to overcome all this. Why are you still wearing a hood in the sunlight?"

"He showed me the fountain, but I'm still drinking from it. There's a well inside of me, but sometimes I want a drink that's faster, or easier, and I take what I can get. There's a part of me that's not a vampire anymore, and there's this other part that still wants to be, sometimes. So every day I have to get a little sunshine, because sunlight doesn't kill vampires, it just burns the vampire out and leaves the human stronger. But until all the work is done I'm a vampire with a tan." She took her hood off and winced in the sunlight. "It hurts. But it's better than a half-life in the dark."

I didn't really get it. I didn't understand what she meant, not fully, and it made me nervous to go check on my pet werewolf. So I said my good-byes and walked through the front room and waved to Roberto as I walked past. As I walked out the door I saw a small pile of wooden stakes in the corner of the room, and I wondered if Lara was in more trouble than she had made clear. Like maybe she was thinking about making the question of whether she was dead or alive a little easier, a little clearer. But I pushed that thought down and away and trotted over to Luther's house.

I almost stopped to check in on the wife and kids, but a quick look at my watch told me that the kids were probably doing the snack ritual of the afternoon, which involves the children begging for snacks, rejecting whatever is offered to them, and then complaining about their day until they finally take the offered snack and are then given sufficient energy not to be upset about all of life anymore. My presence mostly just adds an extra step, the part where I yell at them to stop being so cranky and eat something, and that they can't be too hungry if they won't eat the food put in front of them. I figured we'd all be better off without that, so although I slowed by my house, I didn't stop.

Pretty soon I was knocking on the door, and Luther answered. Or rather, a werewolf answered. A werewolf in a dapper suit and tie, spectacles and a grin on his snout, and a large theological treatise in one hand.

"Greetings, human," he said, and he licked his chops. I choked and tried to step backwards, but he already had me in his claws. "Not by the hair of my chinny chin chin," I managed to squeak as he yanked me into his house and slammed the door shut.

CHAPTER 18

WHO SOOTHES
THE SAVAGE BEAST

WHEN THE DOOR SLAMMED shut behind me, three things crossed my mind. One, I was about to be killed by a savage Lutheran werewolf. Two, perhaps savage was a strong adjective seeing as how this particular wolflike creature was wearing spectacles and a suit. Three, Luther had become positively chatty in his wolf form in comparison to earlier.

"Please don't eat me," I managed to say, hoping this would convey to him the depth of the trouble I felt I was in. But his yellow eyes swept over me before he let me go and picked up a brush from the kitchen table. He started to comb his face.

"I've invited Clarissa to the house," he said, and then paused, as if waiting for some sort of acknowledgment from me. "She should be here any minute, and I would appreciate your support."

"How did you get all . . . normal?"

He sighed. "Your psychologist helped me understand that I am, in fact, a werewolf, and that is not something that can be changed. It can only be lived with, and through behavioral training she has helped me to embrace that fact, allowing me to remain a werewolf but not behave as a werewolf."

"Sort of the equivalent of training a dog not to mark his territory?"

The werewolf frowned, or at least I think he frowned (it's a little hard to tell when someone has a muzzle instead of a human mouth), and said, "I suppose. If that's the unflattering terminology necessary for you to understand my transformation. The important thing is this: when Clarissa arrives I am going to show her that she need not fear me any longer. This will be the first step toward repairing our marriage, and in time we will be reunited. I asked her to bring our daughter, Renata, as well."

The doorbell rang, and Luther's ears perked up. "It's probably your wife," I said. The fact that she rang the doorbell made me sad, somehow. She already looked at this place as Luther's home and not her own. "Maybe I should give you two some space."

His clawed hand grabbed my forearm. "No. If I start to get out of control I need you to reason with me. Help me stay rational."

"How do I do that?"

"It works like this. Imagine there is a man who often sexually harasses his employees at work. He seems unable to control this. However, there is one employee who, although he is alone with her, he would never dream of harassing her. Why? Because his system of interaction with her makes this an unthinkable transaction, because she is his sister. He must be trained to think of all the other female employees as his sisters, do you see? Dr. van Pelt walked me through a similar underpinning for my wife. She showed me that while it's fine for a werewolf to take his base impulses out on a chicken or stray cat, he must never do so to his wife. I need your help to remember this."

The doorbell rang again. "Okay. I'll stay for her sake if not for yours. Shouldn't you let her in?"

He crossed the entryway with the click of claws on hard wood and swung the door open, and there stood his wife, impeccably dressed in a businesslike blazer and dark skirt, her hair perfectly coiffed beneath a small pillbox cap. In her hand was a tiny silver revolver. "I purchased silver bullets for it," she said calmly. Planning ahead! If only I had thought of that instead of trying to melt coins in my kitchen.

Luther stepped back from the doorway, and Clarissa crossed the threshold sideways, keeping her eyes and the pistol trained on him. "Where's Renata?" he asked.

"I didn't bring her, of course. I didn't know what you might do to her. Who's your friend?"

"I'm just the neighbor, and I can let myself out."

"Oh no you don't. I want you here in case my husband tries something violent."

Luther held up his paws in a gesture of surrender. "Clarissa, my love, I invited you over to show you that I have tamed the inner beast. You need not fear me any longer."

She motioned with the gun for him to move into the kitchen, which he did. She stood so that the counter was between her and us, giving her a good shot at either of us before we could get at her. Not that I was going to attack her or anything. I'm just saying that from her point of view it was a good place to go. She was smart. "You're still a wolf. You'll always be a wolf. And sooner or later, a wolf bites. A wolf kills."

"No, Clarissa, this is what I'm learning. I don't need to be that way any longer. I've changed."

I should have kept my mouth shut. But I have this little character flaw. I like to listen to Oregon Public Broadcasting on the radio, follow the news stories, and then drop them into conversations to make me look smarter. Sometimes I might even correct someone if I thought they were saying something that was a little off. Like this. "You know, that's what the people reintroducing wolves in the northwest keep saying, but the ranchers keep saying, 'Those wolves are going to eat my cattle.' Or flocks. Maybe it's just sheep, I don't know. But the point is that as they are reintroducing wolves, the wolves are eating livestock, and the farmers are mad."

Luther's lips curled back, and I saw his long white teeth. A little snarl escaped his lips. I wasn't sure if Clarissa heard it, but it made the hair on my arms stand up. "This is between me and my wife. Keep your mouth shut."

"Your friend makes an excellent point, Luther. Have you really changed? Is it possible? I wonder." She toyed with the gun, as if she were going to set it down. I was nervous. I still had this working theory that silver bullets could kill a person as easily as a werewolf, and I didn't want to test it. It seemed like the laws of physics made the outcome of the experiment reasonably obvious.

But Clarissa was lowering the gun on purpose, watching for his response. "I left Renata with someone. I don't want to tell you who."

"Who?" Luther's voice sounded harsher. I noted with alarm that his pupils had dilated, and his breathing was speeding up. "I told you to bring her. You said you would bring her."

"Yes. I had second thoughts when I considered what this conversation would likely be about."

His claws were clacking against each other, and my palms were getting sweaty. I moved a little closer to him, thinking I could knock him down and give Clarissa a chance to run if he went wild. I said, "Remember what Dr. van Pelt was teaching you about being a werewolf without acting like a werewolf?"

"What do you mean, Clarissa? What is this conversation about?"

She turned the pistol absentmindedly in her hands. The way she did it looked practiced, like she had conversations with people while holding pistols all the time. I knew she could hurt him in a moment, just by wanting to do it. It was as simple as point and shoot. "I've been talking to my minister, and he thinks we should go to counseling."

A rough laugh forced its way from Luther's throat. "Since when did you go to church, Clarissa? Since when did you listen to ministers? Or counselors?"

"Since I left here, Luther. I wanted to talk to someone who understood our situation." She paused and tapped the barrel of the pistol against the counter. "I mean really understood what you struggle with. Someone who had seen it firsthand."

Luther's breathing went from hoarse straight to panting. His feet looked like he was doing some stuttering dance as he made small motions toward Clarissa, then stumbled back. His body was curving, hunching over. "What have you done? Who did you talk to? Who has Renata?"

I stepped closer to him, but he didn't notice. His eyes were locked on her, and a low rumbling growl was coming from his chest.

"Luther, remember what the counselor said. Breathe deeply and think about her instructions. It is unacceptable to behave in certain ways, and you can overcome your desire to—"

With a sound more animal than human, Luther swung a hairy fist at me. I turned my head just in time for it to connect behind my ear and send me spinning to the linoleum. I shook it off and pulled myself up to see the married couple standing feet from each other, the werewolf crouched to spring and his wife waiting with her arm extended, her face twisted in an unreadable grimace somewhere between triumph and pity.

She kept the gun pointed with admirable calm, as if she had been here before, as if she had stared down the wolf for years. Maybe she had. "I left Renata with your father," she said, and Luther leapt at her, his claws extended and fangs jutting from his open mouth. I had just enough time to leap toward him and hit him with my shoulder, knocking him into the pantry door, and both of us ended up on the floor, a cabinet of dishes exploding onto the floor around us. Luther didn't stop. His claws scrabbled against the tile, and he strangled out threats toward his wife while I did everything I could to stop him, my full weight on his back and my arms around his neck, choking for all I was worth.

Clarissa hadn't moved. She held the gun for a long moment at Luther's face. "Did you really want our daughter to see this?"

"I can't hold him much longer."

"Or did you want her here for leverage? Did you want to hurt her? Did you think I couldn't stop you?" She waved the gun at him.

His legs were strong, and I could feel him breaking free. I tried to get a better grip around his neck, but I could feel him wheezing in the air even though I was pulling with all my strength. "Clarissa, he's breaking free. I can't—" Luther bucked backward, knocking me into the pantry again. I winced and lost my grip. He made it three steps before I was back on him again, this time with him splayed out on the floor enough that I could more easily slow his forward motion. But it didn't matter. Clarissa grabbed an unbroken dish from the cabinet and brought it down on his head. It shattered into a thousand shards, and he howled, a savage and startling sound that set my heart racing so hard I thought it might crawl through my skin.

"You want to find a cure, Luther?" She held the gun up so he could see it clearly. She set it on the counter. "Here's the cure. But you're not man enough to take it." She turned and walked away, her heels clicking as she walked to Luther's front door, opened it, and slammed it behind her. Luther relaxed until I did, then bolted for the door. I skidded after him down the hallway, but he turned and tore into me with his claws. It burned, and I fell aside as he burst through the front door. Clarissa's car was already gone, but Luther ran around the perimeter of his yard, howling.

I got to my feet, bruised and bloody. I put my arm across my side and stepped outside, then walked back to my house, my feet impossibly heavy. Luther didn't try to stop me or even acknowledge me. The howling carried on most of the night, punctuated by the sound of breaking glass. More than once I thought about the pistol on the counter and wondered if Luther was thinking about it too. I wasn't sure if Luther was capable of rational thought at all right now and knew it would have to wait for morning light.

I did not sleep well that night. Nothing could calm me. I kept getting up to check on the kids, and every time I looked through their doorway and saw the two of them rolled up in their blankets I thought of that wolf across the street, and the vampire, and a whole world full of frightening things and wondered how long I could keep them safe. In bed, I put my arm out to make sure Krista was beside me. I put my hand on her swollen belly and felt the baby move. I dreamed about a lost child, lonely, crying in a shopping mall, but no one would help him. Embarrassed, all the shoppers walked past him, turning their faces away until all the child could see was an unending parade of pant legs and nylons and shopping bags. He crawled beneath a clothes rack and found a tiny silver bullet. He put it in his mouth and held it there for a long moment before he swallowed it and lay down to sleep.

A wEREwoLf sHAREs HIs THouqHTs AbouT LovE

The primary idiocy of Christianity, and one that is repeated ad nauseam, is that God loves people. God loves me. God loves you. God loves everyone except for the people I hate, of course, but that is another topic entirely.

The idea that some supreme being, one who is capable of creating the complex world of atomic particles and the simple parade of adaptability that we call life, takes time from the millions of undiscovered countries among the galaxies to take interest in my life can only be a philosophy of enormous hubris. At least the gods of Greece and Rome took interest only in the most exceptional of men, but Christians will say that God is equally concerned for the Queen of England and the door-to door salesman trying to convince me that his cleaning solution is superior to the

NIGHT OF THE LIVING DEAD CHRISTIAN

store brand. I find this concept of a loving God not only unlikely, not merely laughable, but offensive.

It comes from a basic misunderstanding of what love could possibly be. For is not love based in some way upon the excellent qualities of the object of our love? For instance, I did not fall in love with my wife because of the unattractive way she flosses her teeth. On the contrary, it was the graceful way she walked, the soft-spoken way she corrected her graduate students, the clear-minded approach she took to any obstacle that dared raise itself against her, the mischievous look in her eye when she looked up from her grading, saw me, and smoothed back the dark hair dangling in her face.

Before you raise your objections, allow me to point out that all your praise songs, all your worshipful hymns have a great deal to do with why God is "worthy" of our affections, why he is great, his name is wonderful, he is stronger than an army, his love is wider than the sea, and hyperbolic sentiments cannot exaggerate his über-hyperbolic nature.

Thus we come to the likewise ridiculous Christian sentiment that he has "chosen" or "elected" us to be in relationship with him, and that he loves us and adopts us as his progeny. It is like saying I have tipped over an anthill and selected certain ones of them to be my children. Not merely that, but I have chosen to sacrifice my human child so their accursed anthill can be spared destruction, and that I am making this handful of ants the heirs of my vast estate—of my house, my car, my food, my clothes, my money. Certainly this comparison does not even begin to scratch the surface of the ridiculous claims of the Christian faith.

I have spoken with certain Christians who tell me it is not for me to decide who is worthy of God's love, and on this point I must concede, for we all make our choices, some good and some ill, and none can tell my heart whom to love. I will point out, however, that for an infinite being to choose someone such as myself for loving relationship reveals a weakness of heart or softness of mind that categorizes this God in some section of imbecility. I am not a person worthy of affection.

My wife, who at one time loved me dearly, soon learned that my foibles far outweigh my virtues. I can only applaud her decision to take our daughter and abandon me. It is what I would do myself if there were some way to divorce myself from my self. I am a wretched creature, and full of evil.

I suppose it has become clear to you at this point that I struck my wife. I struck her, in fact, with the full force of my weight behind the blow, which turned more toward slap than punch, and yet left her bleeding beneath the skin. I did this because she had done some small thing that crossed my purposes. It need not matter what it was, for the fact is that I would have found some excuse by the day's end to hit her.

This is bad enough in itself, though you could make excuses for me, I'm sure: I was tired, and it had been a long day, and there are urges that I try to fight but cannot. And after all, I love my wife. I should be forgiven, you might say. We can all be forgiven, you might say. I think not. It seems to me I should be punished, and most severely. I cannot, in fact, think of a punishment severe enough for such a transgression.

And it gets worse than my actions alone. For instance, while I could dwell on the regret and apologies, the profuse guilt and torment that followed the blow, I cannot deny that in the moment itself there was a feeling of profound satisfaction, that I enjoyed the look of terror on her face, that the sound of my knuckles on her cheek created a blossoming certainty of power and superiority that I drank in like nectar, and that my first thought was to strike her again. I could tell you that it was, in fact, the first time I had struck her, but not the first time I had considered it, and I could tell you that I instantly wondered what I could do to stop myself from doing it again while quietly planning to make it a habit. I wondered what it would be like to strike my daughter.

No doubt you recoil from these frank admissions, but I suspect you recoil because you recognize them and have buried your own similar stories too deeply to acknowledge me as a mirror. Not to say that you desire to strike your spouse, or even that you have a spouse. But perhaps you like the tiny thrill of pocketing something that does not belong to you, or you enjoy taking a small bit of another person's vitality in a one-night stand and then slipping out the door. Perhaps you merely enjoy the small barbs and carefully destructive words that can cause a coworker to look like an imbecile and you his superior, or you enjoy sharing information that is not yours with someone else, or giving attention to a man who is not your husband because he makes you feel for one moment like someone cares.

The fact of the human condition is that we are all more the villain than the hero and that the speech that the Bard put in the mouth of Don John is most nearly reflective of our inner selves: "If I had my mouth, I would bite; if I had my liberty, I would do my liking: in the meantime let me be that I am and seek not to alter me."

If a famine came I would snatch the last crust of bread from a child. I would gladly push women and children into the icy water to win the last seat on a lifeboat. In a gas chamber, I would be the one at the pinnacle of the pyramid of bodies gasping for the last clean breath. Unless it was you, of course, who did those things. Unless it was you.

Thus the concept of the loving God begins to show its ragged edges. Theologians speak of people who are "totally depraved" and incapable of doing any good thing without the direct intervention of this magnificent loving deity. To which I say, why should he bother? What possible virtue could we exhibit that would cause him to take one nanosecond from one day in all of history to expend one billionth of his energy or attention on us? Why not let us chafe and war and rape and corrupt one another over the course of a few decades and then sweep up the bones? What possible reason could he have to save us? What sane motivation would cause him to intervene at all, let alone make sacrifices for us? What God would care for a ragtag collection of puking, mewling, damaged creatures who want nothing more than to be the kings and queens of their own piles of refuse? Let them rot, I say, as any intelligent creature before or after me would say.

And here is the final evidence that we have invented God for ourselves. Who could love us other than we ourselves? No one. We have invented a being to love us despite our depravities. As Nietzsche said, "Is man only a blunder of God, or God only a blunder of man?" I don't believe there is a third choice, not if we must choose between no God or a loving one. A loving God is insipid and cruel. Put us out of our misery. Don't prolong it, don't encourage it, don't say that there is something of worth and raise our hopes when there is no hope in this world, no, for we cannot change in a hundred years, and in less time than that we will be dust, thank God. Then, at least, we will be little more than an annoyance to be swept out of the houses of our twisted descendants. But there will be no talk of love any longer, for no one, not even God, cares one whit about a handful of dust.

CHAPTER 19

THE NOT-SO-SECRET LAIR

I WOKE IN THE MORNING afraid to go to Luther's house. Instead, I did some things I hadn't done for several weeks. I got up and helped the kids get ready for school. Which, at their age, has more to do with harassing them endlessly to get themselves ready than with actually getting them ready. Two bowls of oatmeal, two sack lunches, and a five-minute walk through the crisp morning cold, and they were both delivered to their daily scholastic impartations. I walked home slowly, wondering whether I should go to Luther's or leave well enough alone.

The Hibbs 3000 stepped up alongside me without saying anything. I looked at him sidelong, but since he wasn't saying anything I figured I wouldn't say anything either. We walked in lockstep for several blocks before he said, "Dr. Culbetron will not like this."

"Dr. Culbetron won't like us walking together?"

"No." Hibbs stopped by the roses outside my fence. They're a kind of antique rose that blooms only for a short time once a year, and every inch of the bush is covered in thorns. There weren't any flowers on them, but Hibbs bent over and sniffed at the thorn-covered plants.

"What are you doing?"

Hibbs sniffed at the thorns again before saying, "Stopping to smell the roses."

I scratched my chin. "There aren't any roses on there."

"Dr. Culbetron told me to stop and smell the roses once in a while. He said I am working too hard." He stood up straight and glanced around the neighborhood. "These are roses, are they not?"

"Yeah, they're rosebushes. And why does a robot need to work less?" Hibbs tore a branch off the rosebush. "What are you doing?"

"I want to give roses to my special someone."

"Hibbs, do you have a screw loose? You're a robot. Are you in love with a coffee machine? And what is it that Culbetron won't like?"

Hibbs sighed and handed me a folded piece of paper. Written in neat print at the top it said MAP TO THE SECRET LAIR OF DR. CULBETRON. I gaped at the map in disbelief. "You guys have a secret lair? And you didn't invite me?"

Hibbs said, completely devoid of compassion, "From our brief acquaintance we have learned three things: One, you are incapable of keeping secrets. Two, the doctor believes you would ruin some of his experiments. Three, we like to have a break from you sometimes."

"I can't believe you guys have a secret lair." The picture that leapt into my head of a life-size mock-up of a dinosaur, an enormous penny, and lots of cool planes and cars and trophies and computers almost made me well up with tears.

"Now you possess a map." Hibbs cocked his head at the folded paper and continued collecting stems until he had a thorny bouquet of twelve. "Do not tell the doctor how you discovered it."

"Why are you giving this to me now?"

"Our experiments may be of interest to Luther. We deal primarily with human transformation."

I shuddered. "Like turning people into flies."

"Precisely the opposite."

I shuddered again. "Ugh. Turning flies into people? That's worse."

"No. Turning monsters into people."

It took a moment for that to sink in. Hibbs and Culbetron had been working on experiments on human transformation, the very thing we were looking for. "Great! I'll go get Luther." I trotted across the street to Luther's house. The door was closed, but I turned the handle and it gave way beneath my touch. The front part of the house was spotless, and I walked back toward the kitchen, keeping my eyes open in case my feral neighbor decided to ambush and eat me. I found Luther sitting on a kitchen stool, leaning on the long handle of a mop, broken glass still scattered around him. His face looked like it had been caught in a gravity well and pulled out of shape. He scarcely bothered to respond when I explained about Dr. Culbetron's Secret Lair. I tried to get him excited about the life-size dinosaur, and when he seemed disinterested I suggested there might be a giant cavern made out of crystals, or maybe the hideout was inside a satellite orbiting the earth.

At this point some signs of life stirred in Luther. "And how, pray tell, are we going to get to the satellite? Perhaps we should just go have a picnic on the moon."

I waved the paper under his nose. "Doesn't it sound fun? Come on. It'll be an adventure."

He stood reluctantly. I started for the door, but he grabbed my forearm and pulled me back. "Who you saw last night, that's not who I am. Do you understand?"

I took a deep breath. "You mean when you tried to get your claws into your wife?"

"That's right. I'm not that person."

The gun was gone from the counter, and I wondered where it had gotten off to. "Who are you then, Luther? And who was that last night? People are always doing things and saying afterward, 'Oh, that's not like me.' Except that it is like them. It's precisely like them, because they are the ones who did it. You are that person, not just the pleasant person you can be when you are well fed and have had enough sleep and aren't angry at anyone. It's still you when you bite and snap, it's still you when you try to hurt someone." I lifted my shirt and showed him the laceration from his claws that still burned there. "You're the one who did that, Luther. So let's stop talking about who you aren't and talk about who you are. And if that's not who you want to be, then let's see what we can do about changing you into someone better."

"But shouldn't I love myself the way I am? Shouldn't I embrace me and be at peace with who I am?"

I sighed. "If you're satisfied with who you are, Luther, then that's fine. But you've already told me you want to be something more. And Borut is still hunting people like you. If you can live with that, that's your business. But don't tell me it's not who you are."

Luther flattened the map out on the counter and studied it closely. "This map had best not lead us to my father's church, or I will be angry. I don't like to be deceived."

"I don't think so. It's in downtown Vancouver. In fact, I recognize the address. That's strange. I've been there a hundred times before. That's the address for Ice Cream Renaissance."

Luther got to his feet. "So your friends think it would be funny to tell me that ice cream can help make me a better man? I am tired of jokes. Doesn't anyone care enough to tell me the truth about how I can be changed?"

"Relax. I'm sure there's more to it than that. But maybe they have a wolfsbane flavor this month."

Luther's face twisted like he had eaten an entire lemon. "Ha. I'll buy you a scoop of hemlock flavor if they have any."

I stood silently for a moment, realizing that Luther had become, in a very short time, my friend. I felt badly for the way his wife had treated him the night before, even though he deserved it and probably worse. But still, he had invited her to the house in good faith, wanting to show her that he had made steps toward health, and she had purposely torn him apart. I wanted to help him find the peace I had found myself, and though he wasn't interested, I wanted to try to explain to him again that following Jesus didn't have to mean zombified Christianity, that it could be something with real, vibrant, overflowing life. Not just a list of rules or a mantra of creeds, but something that could actually change him, something that could alter the way he interacted with the human race. It seemed that his father had effectively closed that door for him. I worried that in his despair over the loss of his family and his worsening condition, and the stress of Borut being after him, Luther might do something desperate. "Luther. Where's the gun your wife left here?"

Luther's attention wandered to me, like a man coming out of deep meditation. His eyes took a moment to focus, and when he finally heard my question he said, "Oh, that. I took care of it."

"Took care of it? Threw it away? Locked it up?"

"It's somewhere safe."

"I think I should probably hold on to it."

Luther laughed. "To keep in your house with your pregnant wife and two children? I don't think so. Besides, with your record of clumsiness and ineptitude, the likelihood of your shooting me by mistake is much higher than my chance of shooting myself on purpose." He clapped me on the shoulder. "Let's go see what your idiot friends have cooked up. And if nothing else, you can buy me some wolfsbane ice cream."

I took one last quick glance around the kitchen for the pistol before I agreed.

CHAPTER 20

BORN-AGAIN ICE CREAM

RENAISSANCE MEANS REBIRTH, or at least that's what they told me in my college humanities class, and probably in high school history and possibly in grade school. And ice cream means a cool and tasty snack which should be consumed and often is, and in my experience, is a snack of such perfect excellence that even the lactose intolerant will tolerate it for brief but glorious moments. When you put these words together to create Ice Cream Renaissance, you have created something of unrivaled splendor. Perhaps a place where ice cream itself will be reborn? Or where I can be reborn through ice cream? Be honest, this is something that you must experience for yourself.

Ice Cream Renaissance is a little shop on Main Street

in downtown Vancouver, Washington. (I should point out that this city is different from Vancouver, Canada, which is a source of endless confusion for certain people. A major airline once told me I couldn't use my credit card to buy a ticket because I was using a credit card from outside the United States. When I explained to the help desk that Washington was, indeed, inside the United States, I was told that their research department would look into it and get back to me. It took three days to get my plane tickets.)

The shop is small but clean, with reproductions of Renaissance paintings on the walls and tables, a stack of games in the corner encouraging you to stay and enjoy yourself, and blackboards on the walls listing today's flavors of ice cream: Honey Vanilla, Oregon Strawberry, Bittersweet Chocolate Love Affair, Peanut Butter Blitz, Pumpkin Pie, and on and on. One of the inexplicable things about the place is how it can have such excellent, handmade ice cream and pie and be so inexpensive. I ordered my usual, a scoop of Oregon Strawberry with fresh whipped cream, and Luther got the Sundae Madness, which came on a plate that immediately declared that he would not be able to finish it, but that didn't stop us both from trying.

I was about a third of the way through my ice cream when a tall figure in a lab coat hurried by, and I shouted, "Dr. Culbetron?"

The man in the lab coat hesitated, and without turning around he said in a high-pitched voice, "You must be mistaken. My name is Dr. . . . Danger."

"Dr. Danger?"

"That's right. Now if you'll excuse me, I must be going."

"To your Secret Lair?"

The good doctor stopped again, then turned to face us. With a deadly calm he said, "So. You've discovered my Secret Lair at last. I knew it was only a matter of time. I suppose I will have to move all my things to the Even-More-Secret Lair, or perhaps even to the Lair That Is Slightly More Secret Than the More-Secret Lair."

He put his finger in my ice cream and then put his finger in his mouth. "Strawberry." He picked up my ice cream and spoon and started eating it absentmindedly. "Very well. You may as well come along and see the Lair before we move out of it, now that it's the Not-So-Secret Lair."

We followed him toward the back of the store, and he pointed out a section of black and white tiles on the floor and instructed us to pull up on them. We did as he said, and they came away to reveal a short drop into an underground tunnel. I jumped in first, followed by Luther and then Culbetron. We followed the tunnel about twenty yards before it widened enough for us to stand up straight, and then it followed a bend and I could see light ahead where it widened again into a large cavern. The Hibbs 3000 stood with his back to us, wearing a white lab coat and holding a beaker of what looked like blood. Discarded around the room were manikins and various pieces of robots—arms, legs, and heads. There were giant liquid-filled vats with strange creatures floating in them, and space-age devices shooting out electricity, and some chains on one wall, and one of those wallpaper murals that made the far wall look like we were inside a castle with the moon shining outside, surrounded by the arched stone window of a parapet. To my left was something that looked like a laser cannon. There was a small blue sticky note on it with the words TIME MACHINE—PLEASE DO NOT TOUCH.

"Gasp," Hibbs said. "I am surprised. How did you find us? The shock, it is shocking me."

Culbetron scowled. "I already know it was you, Hibbs. For shame."

Hibbs frowned back at Culbetron. "I merely thought the Clockwork Project might be of use to Luther. Or perhaps our current cloning endeavor."

The place, frankly, looked shabby, like someone had dug a hole in the ground under a building and then moved in a bunch of amazing scientific equipment. "How did you guys make this place?"

Culbetron turned back to his beakers and Bunsen burners. "We dug a hole in the ground and then moved in our fancy scientific equipment."

I walked between two long metal tables crammed full of strange creatures and eyeballs in jars and disassembled video game systems. "I thought there would at least be a life-size dinosaur."

Culbetron jumped as if he had been burned. "Hibbs, where is our dinosaur?"

With a sudden lurch Hibbs quickly began to look under

tables, moving piles of paper and scooting boxes around until he proudly held up a small skeletal statue of a dinosaur, about four inches tall, but stretching a foot-and-a-half wide because of its long tail and neck. *"Fruitadens haagarorum.* We call her Fruity."

I crossed my arms. "That's not a dinosaur, that's a chicken. You know, guys, this Secret Lair is really disappointing. It's more like a clubhouse or storage facility."

Culbetron rolled his eyes. "That's why we don't invite you to things."

"It's significantly better than a car in someone's driveway," Hibbs said.

Luther cleared his throat. "I don't mean to interrupt, but I wonder about your so-called Clockwork Project and how it might be useful to me."

Culbetron's eyes lit up, and he motioned to Hibbs, who joined him at the far end of the large room. There was a small metal door in the side of the impacted dirt, and they motioned us closer. "Behind this door you shall find a collection of creations that will baffle and amaze you. The Hibbs 3000 and I have been working hard to recreate some of the greatest minds and characters of centuries past. People who have made a difference, people who have done amazing things. We have focused particularly on people who have made tremendous moral decisions or been people of exemplary character. We have taken all their known writings and used those to create robot versions of each of them." He flung the door open. "BEHOLD! The Clockwork Project!"

Luther and I both gasped when the door was flung open, more out of shock than wonder. When the door swung wide enough for us to see inside, it looked something like the wax workshop at Madame Tussauds must look. There were half-built, nearly recognizable people. Gandhi's torso sat on the floor, and his head was cradled in Abraham Lincoln's arms ten feet away. Mother Teresa was there, and a large number of people I did not recognize.

"We only have enough power to run one at a time," Hibbs said apologetically, holding up a massive battery made from several car batteries wired together. Hibbs is very strong. "Who would you like to talk with?"

Luther said, without a moment's hesitation, "I want to talk to Jesus." I could see the anticipation on his face, even though we all knew it wasn't the real Jesus, just a mocked-up, robotic version of him.

"Jesus it is," Culbetron said, and he stepped into the room, Hibbs just behind him, and started working on a manikin in a robe and sandals.

CHAPTER 21

CLOCKWORK JESUS

"What is this monstrosity?"

Standing before us was our requested member of the Clockwork Project, Clockwork Jesus. He wore what appeared to be a leftover shepherd's robe from a Christmas pageant, and he walked with a strange, stuttering limp. His face looked like the Terminator's face. It was silver and unyielding, with a small grate, which I assumed housed a speaker so he could talk to us.

Culbetron stuck out his lip in a pout. "Making robots in this time period is extremely difficult, especially when your lab is a hole in the ground."

"What about Hibbs? He looks like an ordinary person. Except for the unnaturally wide shoulders and the extremely tight T-shirt."

Hibbs and Culbetron did not answer this question. Instead, Culbetron said, "We've downloaded every known translation of the Bible into the Clockwork Jesus. You can ask him any question you like, and his sophisticated microprocessors and fuzzy logic sensors will work hard to give you an appropriate answer, straight out of the Bible. What translation would you like him set on?"

Luther immediately said, "I believe I will take the New Revised Standard Version, which is most popular among Lutheran ministers."

"That's such a formal translation," I said. "Jesus will sound like a, I don't know, an accountant or something." Nothing against accountants. I like accountants. "Let's do *The Message* or the New Living Translation or one of those that sounds like Hawaiian slang, something that will make it more interesting to listen to."

"You would dare sacrifice precision of translation for accessibility? This is precisely why you weak-chinned secondary Protestants are so theologically infirm."

"I happen to think the whole point of translating is to make the Bible accessible. And so did Martin Luther." I squinted at him. "Martin Luther went out among the people to make sure his translation matched the everyday talk in the marketplace." I threw my hands up. "Okay, okay, let's meet halfway and use the New International Version."

"Halfway?" Luther tried to get a sentence out of his mouth but sputtered uncontrollably for several seconds before doing it. His face started to sprout fur, and I could see his fangs dropping in. "If you'd like to meet halfway then we should use the English Standard Version."

"Do you really think something like the English Standard Version is going to be completely intelligible to someone on the street? It's formal too."

"Perhaps you merely think it is too formal because you are not sufficiently educated to articulate a fully formed grammatical construct in such a way that your sentences become freighted with complexity and connotative as well as denotative meaning."

"And maybe you're just dumb because you're a big old dumb werewolf." When I said that, Luther gasped and leaned backward, trying to put distance between us. "I'm sorry, Luther. I shouldn't have said that, and I didn't mean it."

He looked away and mumbled, "*Wes das Herz voll ist, des geht der Mund über.*"

Hibbs cleared his throat and said, "I have the perfect Bible version for you two, one that you'll have to agree on." He stepped behind the Clockwork Jesus and adjusted something at the back of its neck. "Go ahead and ask him a question."

Luther leapt up and asked, "Which English Bible translation is the best?"

The Clockwork Jesus whirred and clanked and said, "το πνευμα εστιν το ζωοποιουν, η σαρξ ουκ ωφελει ουδεν. τα ρηματα εγω λαλω υμιν πνε μα εστιν και ζωη εστιν."

"Oh, very funny, Hibbs. Take it off of Greek, will you? We don't speak Greek."

"Precisely," Hibbs said. "You two argue over which

translation is best, most accurate, or most accessible. If you care so much, then go learn Greek and Hebrew. If the Holy Spirit really empowers the Bible, then what are you so worried about? Do you think he can speak through the NIV but not the ESV, or vice versa? Do you think he can't use a paraphrase to say what he needs to say to his readers? The fact is, all those translations are the Scriptures. They have different styles and different purposes, and yes, depending on what you are using them for, one might be more appropriate than another. But you should stop fighting over translations so much that it prevents you from reading the Scriptures.

"I'm going to set Clockwork Jesus to use multiple translations." He monkeyed around at the robot's neck again and then motioned for us to continue. "There." Hibbs slapped his hands together. "Make your questions as specific as possible. It's a computer, not a living thing." I looked carefully at Hibbs. It seemed to me that his usual way of speaking had changed. Hibbs was not what he seemed. I was starting to wonder if he was a robot at all.

Luther seemed nervous. He stood close to the Clockwork Jesus and said, "A lot of people say different things about how to be saved. How to go to Heaven, or how to be saved from this broken world, or how to overcome all the evil in my own life. And I suppose that is my question: What do I have to do to get eternal life?"

I smiled to myself. Luther had asked a simple question, one that had an answer easily rattled off by church kids by the time they are ten. Salvation is a mysterious process created by a God so far beyond us intellectually that to compare our intellects to his would be to compare Stephen Hawking to a pebble, but you can boil it down to a few simple points with no trouble. God loves us. There are plenty of verses for that, and I knew the Clockwork Jesus could reel them off. The old standard, of course, would be God loved the world so much that he sent his only Son that whoever believes in him need not die, but can live forever. It's not just that God loves us but the fact that we do sinful things (wrong things—that we mess up morally), and the Scriptures on that are clear as well. The paycheck for doing wrong is death. No exceptions. And then we get into the whole idea that God desires us to live. Jesus came so we could have life, and have more of it, and we have to believe in our hearts and confess with our mouths that Jesus is Lord and we will be saved. So the computer in Clockwork Jesus had a lot of options for how to answer the question, "What must I do to be saved?"

It whirred its gears for a few brief seconds, and then it said, "You know the commandments: 'Be faithful in marriage. Do not murder. Do not steal. Do not tell lies about others. Respect your father and mother.'"

Wait. What? "What is going on here, Culbetron? That's your robot's answer if someone comes up and asks out of the blue, 'What does it take to get eternal life?' That's not very helpful. It sounds like salvation through works. Something's wrong with this machine."

Culbetron made tiny calming motions with his eyebrows.

"We're still working out the bugs. Just keep talking to it, and it will give you a clear answer."

Luther sneered at the Clockwork Jesus in disgust. "I suppose I already missed my chance, then. I cannot imagine that my marriage meets the eternal life requirements. It's in complete shambles."

I pointed a finger at Clockwork Jesus angrily. "Well, I've done all those things since I was just a kid. Is that all you have to say? Don't you want to say anything about repentance or theology?"

Clockwork Jesus turned its head toward me and said, "There is still one thing you haven't done. Sell all your possessions and give the money to the poor, and you will have treasure in heaven. Then come, follow me."

"It has a screw loose. That's a terrible answer to the question. Luther, ask again." I hoped that Culbetron's Frankenstein Jesus was just warming up.

"Very well. Clockwork Jesus, what must I do to receive eternal life?"

Those bright, lamp-lit clockwork eyes turned on me, and he said, "What is written in the Law? How do you read it?"

He turned it over to me. I licked my lips and looked at Luther. This was my big chance to lay it out so he would understand. But Clockwork Jesus had hemmed me in a bit by putting the question in the context of the Law. So I had to look to God's commandments and rules to the people. What was in there that would be comprehensive enough to answer the question? There wasn't really a rule that said, "Repent and believe." So I thought it over and came down to the big two, the commandments that Jesus had once said were the most important commandments of all. "Love the Lord your God with all your heart, all your soul, all your strength, and all your mind, and love your neighbor as you love yourself."

The robot nodded and said, "Thou hast answered right: this do, and thou shalt live."

Luther sighed. "So what we do is more important than what we believe. Or so it seems."

"That's not the whole picture," I said. "Tell him, Hibbs. Scripture is full of instructions about what to believe and the importance of believing in Christ to get to God."

"Clockwork Jesus is programmed to give the most direct response from Jesus' answers. He doesn't go into Paul's letters or the other letters to the churches. He's purely the words of Jesus."

I shook my head in frustration. "You make it sound like Jesus just cared about us following some rules, though, and that's simply not true. Why doesn't he quote from John when Jesus said, 'Whoever believes in the Son of Man is not condemned, but whoever does not believe stands condemned already because he has not believed in the name of God's one and only Son'?"

Culbetron put his hand on my shoulder. "You have to ask the Clockwork Jesus very specific questions if that's the answer you want. Is he not giving you the answers you want when he answers your questions the same way that Jesus did?"

Luther rubbed his chin. "Clockwork Jesus, in the passage

that Matt just quoted, does Jesus say anything about our actions, or is it only that we must believe in the Son of Man?"

Clockwork Jesus paused for the barest moment before saying, "This is the verdict: Light has come into the world, but men loved darkness instead of light because their deeds were evil. Everyone who does evil hates the light and will not come into the light for fear that his deeds will be exposed. But whoever lives by the truth comes into the light, so that it may be seen plainly that what he has done has been done through God."

We all sat silently for a moment, and I tried to figure out how this all fit together. So what I believe matters— that much seemed obvious from what I had quoted, if not from Clockwork Jesus' quotes. But it seemed that Jesus didn't spend a lot of time going into the details. In fact, he spent a lot of time talking about our actions. But could our actions alone save us? Not if we had to believe in the Son of Man. But could our beliefs alone save us? Well. That's what I had been taught. That's what I believed.

Luther seemed distant, and Hibbs was working on something at a back table. Culbetron held up a finger and said, "We do have another project we've been working on that attempts to address this very question." He pointed out a wide table that was covered in boiling liquids in strange, wandering glass tubes, and a few white, round crackers and small goblets of what appeared to be wine.

"Communion," I said. "You think Communion is the answer to the problem?"

MATT MIKALATOS

Culbetron laughed. "No, not at all."

Hibbs said, "We stole these from a Catholic church."

Culbetron cackled gleefully. "Indeed. And as you know, the Catholics believe that the wafer and wine become the actual body and blood of Christ." He held up a wafer reverently. "And Hibbs and I started talking, and we thought . . . what if we were to use a wafer from Catholic Communion and we *cloned Jesus?*"

I gasped. "You're insane, Doctor! Also, I think you misunderstand the Catholic doctrine of transubstantiation, because I'm pretty sure it can't be used to clone a living Jesus."

Culbetron's face fell. "I thought that might be. The process has been . . . inconclusive." He held up a petri dish that looked like someone had chewed up the wafer and wine and put it into the dish.

"I know you were trying to do something good, Culbetron, like make a clone of Jesus that we could study and learn from, but do you really think that would have worked?"

Culbetron shrugged. "You never know until you try. First rule of science." He looked around for someone to back him up. "Second rule of science? Third? I don't remember."

Luther stood and looked at his watch. "Gentlemen. I have decided it's time to try a church again. Not the zombie church, of course."

Culbetron looked up suddenly as if he had lost something, and then he spun around, his hand shading his eyes as if he was peering off into the distance. "Speaking of zombies, where's Robert?"

I pretended to look around. "Um. I have him power washing the siding on my house today. It's teaching him spiritual discipline. Mr. Miyagi style."

Luther closed his eyes with a pained look, but eventually managed to pry them open again and said, "Not, as I say, the zombie church." As he said it, a ridge of wolf hair sprouted along his forearms, and his cheek twitched involuntarily. "I think it is time I pay a visit to my father."

CHAPTER 22

YOU'RE NOT MY FATHER!
NO! IT'S NOT TRUE!
I'LL NEVER JOIN YOU!

I DON'T KNOW WHAT I was expecting The Shelter Lutheran Church of Vancouver to look like. There are so many styles of churches in the US these days that it could have been anything from a warehouse with a sea of parking to a glass tower with only one usable level to a rented-out high school gymnasium. But it was, in fact, a middle-sized chapel that had been built in a valley created by a few nearby hills, with houses perched on the edges and looking down on it. A profusion of flowers and trees gave the whole place the look of a Thomas Kinkade painting, complete with soft light and the vibrant pop of color from the flora. In other words, it looked like a place that had nothing to do with the grime and filth of the world we live in, like you would never need to dust or sweep the porch there, like weeds wouldn't dare to grow in the flower beds. It looked like the last place you would go to get answers about taming a werewolf or killing a zombie horde. It looked like the sort of place where you might hit your thumb with a hammer and then smile and say, "What a silly goose I am!" then shake your head ruefully and get back to work while bluebirds poured you a glass of lemonade.

I went in first, and a secretary smiled pleasantly and ushered me into the office of Reverend Martin. His office seemed out of place in the pristine perfection of the church. His desk was enormous, stark, and angular, with a large window that looked inward toward the sanctuary. He was large himself, with wide shoulders and heavy musculature. He had a salt-and-pepper beard that lay in a reverse halo over his chest. But the most shocking decoration was an enormous wolf pelt, staked to the wall over his desk, the fur stained a dark black in places and the face twisted in a canine grimace of pain. Reverend Martin stood when I entered and held out his hand, and I could immediately see how Luther, as a child, would have been overwhelmed, intimidated, even afraid in this man's presence.

I took his hand, and he shook it firmly enough that I could feel the enormous strength of his hands. From the ropy muscles of his forearms I could see he was a man of iron, that his entire person was ramrod straight and unbending. "Mr. Mikalatos. A pleasure to meet you. What can I do for you?"

I took a seat in the small wooden chair in front of his

desk. "Well, Reverend, a couple of things. First of all, I have a bit of zombie trouble."

The reverend laughed. "Tried chain saws? That's the traditional method, but it seems to me you're just making more trouble for yourself, because soon you have piles of disconnected body parts coming at you."

"I can't tell if they're actually dead or alive, so it's unclear whether to kill them or resuscitate them."

Reverend Martin stroked his beard. "That is a conundrum. Hmmm. I'll have to consider that. What is your other problem?"

"I have a friend who is dealing with a werewolf issue." I sat back in the chair. "I hope I'm not weirding you out with all of this."

"I'm a minister. I deal with this sort of thing all the time. Believe me, you won't surprise me with anything you say. Why don't you tell me some more about your 'friend' and his problems."

"It really is my friend, not me. He's my neighbor, and his name is Luther Martin."

Reverend Martin put his hands flat on his desk and leaned toward me. "You *have* surprised me. Luther is my son."

"I know. He's . . . well, he heard that you can help him, but he wanted me to come in and talk to you first. He's not interested in this being some family event. He doesn't want you to touch him or tell him that you missed him."

Martin drummed his fingers on the desk. "He wants a professional appointment, is that it?"

"Yes."

He leaned back and looked out the window, his eyes unfocused and his mouth slack. "Very well, Mr. Mikalatos. Tell Luther he can come in and I will treat him like a stranger, if that's his request."

I walked out to the Secret Lair (my car) to get Luther. He surprised me by asking me to come into the office with him. Every step we took toward that office pained him. His clothes tore around the edges, and we had to stop and take his shoes off because his long, clawed toes were stretching beyond them. He hunched over, panting, and I walked alongside him into his father's office.

Reverend Martin stood up behind his desk, and though a flicker of alarm crossed his face at the site of his lupine son, he said nothing about it, merely gesturing to two chairs and saying, "Gentlemen."

I took my seat, and Luther tried to curl himself into his, with limited success. "Reverend Martin," he said.

"Mr. Martin. How may I help you?"

Luther snapped his teeth. "Don't be smug. I think you know how you can help me. If that pelt over your desk is any indication, you probably intend to skin me before the day is through."

The reverend looked back at the wall and then returned his gaze to us. "I didn't kill that wolf, Luther." He sighed. "We've always misunderstood each other, you and I." He slid his hands along the desk. "What is it you want from me, Luther? What more can I do than what I have done already?"

Luther growled, and his claws dug into the wood of the chair. "What more can you do?" He laughed bitterly. "All you ever did was disapprove of me, Reverend. You looked at what I am, who I am, and you saw only something disgusting, something to be discarded. Oh, you occasionally gave me a book designed to help me 'better' myself, but admit it: when you saw me you saw only your greatest failure."

The reverend sighed again, and his eyes didn't move from his son. He spoke carefully. "I hear what you are saying, Luther. But perhaps you did not hear my question. What do you want me to do for you?"

"Tell me how to get out of this accursed wolf skin!" He yelled this, and it ended in a moan that was half howl.

The minister slapped his hand down on the desk, hard. "You know this already, Luther. I've told you a thousand times. You've read it in books. You've heard it in songs. 'Believe in the Lord Jesus Christ and you shall be saved.' Not only salvation in the sense of some future Heavenly Kingdom, but salvation today. It's that simple, Luther, it has always been that simple. God came to earth as a man, having set aside his power, and lived a perfect life among us. He died on our behalf and was raised again. If we confess with our mouths that Jesus is Lord and believe in our hearts that God raised him from the dead, we will be saved. And if we confess our sins he will be faithful and just to forgive our sins and cleanse us from all unrighteousness."

Luther leapt from his chair, his anger radiating like heat. I leaned back to get away from him. "I've never seen this,

Reverend, never! The Christians I know major on their future reward and minimize their present action. Is it even possible to be 'cleansed' from evil actions? Can I really live a life other than this one? Is there freedom from this misery, or is death the only exit?"

The reverend knocked a stack of papers off his desk. "Oh, Luther. You've never seen anyone live a good life? You've never known a Christian who has lived a righteous life? You're speaking in generalities that are lacking intellectual rigor, as often happens in your screeds."

"I've seen legalists who live their lives in a web of rules that give the appearance of morality, yes. I've seen Christians who specialize in behavioral modification, where the sexual appetite is 'controlled' by telling a man how to look a woman in the eyes, and women are told to wear clothes from another generation because it's somehow their fault if a 'brother stumbles' when he looks at her. Where is the real transformation? If God cleanses from unrighteousness, if he takes a heart of stone and gives a heart of flesh, why are so many 'believers' living lives indistinguishable from their neighbors'? In fact, I take that back. Not indistinguishable, no. They are living lives indistinguishable except for the insufferable arrogance that comes from thinking they know the answer to spiritual questions that others around them have gotten wrong."

"Now you are talking about me, Luther, and not some list of imaginary, generalized Christians."

"Of course I'm talking about you, Father! Who taught me

everything I need to know about Christianity? You! All the theology, all the experiential knowledge comes from you." The minister crumpled, as if he had received a blow. He spoke quietly. "Luther. When I look at you and your brother, I can see myself stamped in you. And I can also see that I wronged you when you were children. I too often expected you to interact as adults. I have no doubt that your spiritual state today is, in some sense, my fault. I am truly sorry for—"

With a terrifying roar Luther leapt across the desk and pummeled his father in the head. The reverend collapsed under the werewolf's weight, and Luther pulled him up by his shirt and yelled, "Do not apologize for my spiritual state! Don't you see that you are showing your disapproval and arrogance even by apologizing?" He hit him again, just as I stood to intervene. "There is something missing! There is something missing!"

A deafening boom exploded behind me, and I fell to the floor. Standing in the doorway was the monster hunter, Borut, a rifle in his hands, smoke still wafting from the barrel. "Vhat is missing, monster, is that you must die. Your time has come, Luther Martin." He grinned. "Your father called to tell me you vere here. And now, volf, you die. Put down your father so no innocents are hurt."

Luther looked at the bloodied mess in his hands and shook his father. "You did this? You called the hunter and told him to find me here? You traitor. I knew you hated me, but never this much."

The minister cracked open a swollen eye and croaked out

in a near whisper, "Unless a seed fall to the ground and die, it cannot live."

The werewolf laughed and reached a clawed hand into his pants pocket. "But I have no intention of dying today." He pulled his hand out and there, clutched in his claws, was the tiny silver pistol from Clarissa. He pointed it at Borut and squeezed off several rounds. I covered my head and heard the sound of breaking glass. There were shouts from Borut, and I could hear growls and angry laughter from deeper within the church. Luther had leapt through a glass barrier that led toward the sanctuary, and I stood in time to see Borut leaping through the remnants of the window. I ran around the desk to Reverend Martin and propped up his head. He was breathing regularly. He opened his eyes again and looked at me. "Help my son," he said. "If he is your friend, help him find who he is looking for."

"You mean *what* he is looking for."

Martin put his hand on mine. "I said what I meant."

I stood and debated for a minute. I didn't want to risk my life over this. I liked Luther, but I wasn't willing to die for him. I heard a shot, and a scream. I picked up the phone from Martin's desk, dialed 911, and told them there were two nuts with guns loose at the church. I left the phone off the cradle and jumped through the window frame. I burst into the sanctuary, and Borut pivoted to train his rifle on my chest. I didn't see Luther anywhere.

CHAPTER 23

THE ONE WHERE I SET
THE CHURCH ON FIRE

Borut turned away in disgust when he saw it was me and trained his rifle on the darkness. The sanctuary was large, filled with pews and with thousands of lit candles. I was momentarily confused by this, as candles seemed a Catholic decoration, but I wasn't familiar with the Lutherans, and maybe this was normal. I waited for my eyes to adjust to the darkness, but when I looked into the dark corners I could see only the deeper blue and the shining thin lights that come from rubbing your eyes in darkness. I couldn't see the werewolf.

"You can't kill him in the church," I said. "Don't you know what sanctuary means? He's safe here."

Borut snorted. "You talk about things you know nothing about. The volf is not safe here. He is not safe anyvhere. Not from me. Not until he is dead."

I heard a scurrying sound in the dark, and Luther's heavy wolf breathing. There was a flash and a popping sound, and Borut fell back against one of the pews, dropping his rifle. A satisfied grunt came from the darkness, and the silver pistol came skidding out on the floor to land at Borut's feet. I ran to Borut, who was clutching his arm. He lifted his palm, and blood flowed freely from his bicep. He gritted his teeth and pulled a long cloth from a pocket in his jacket and wound it around his arm, pulling it tight with his teeth and knotting it. He picked up his rifle with a grunt and used the pew to steady himself when he stood. He didn't say anything, but just walked into the darkness without looking back.

I followed Borut, just in time to see Luther leap up from behind him, tear the rifle from his hands, and send it flying. Borut pulled a knife from his belt and grabbed hold of the werewolf, grappling him to the ground. I saw the flash of the knife's blade in the candlelight and watched it sink into Luther's fur. There was a horrified cry and a shout of triumph, and then I was on top of Borut, tearing him off of Luther, who writhed on the ground, howling. Borut pushed me, and I punched him as hard as I could in his wound from the pistol. His eyes rolled into his head and he almost fell, but he grabbed hold of my shirt and pulled himself up again before shoving me backward with an animal growl.

I stumbled back and knocked into a candelabra, which fell

onto a nearby pew, molten wax and fire covering the cloth. Horrified, I stumbled across the aisle, away from the fire and into another candelabra, which fell onto another pew. "You gotta be kidding me." The flames jumped up as if the pews had been covered in gasoline, and in the orange glare I could see Borut chasing Luther deeper into the recesses of the church. The flames were moving far faster than they should, and I yanked down a banner from the side of the room and used it to try to beat the flames down. But the banner caught on fire, and with a surprised cry I hurled it away from me. It landed near another wall banner, and the fire fled up the side of the building. "Oh, this cannot be good."

I ran to find a phone just as the reverend came limping in, his eyes wide. "What have you done?"

I looked at the burning church building. "Seems sort of self-explanatory."

"Where is my son?"

I pointed into the smoke-filled darkness, and he moved into it with purpose. I stood, torn between calling the fire department and trying to help Luther first. I heard sirens somehow over the crackling flames and remembered I had already called the cops. The fire department would not be far behind.

The flames were getting higher, and smoke alarms throughout the building were beginning to squeal. As I passed the Communion altar, a hand reached out and grabbed my leg. I fell away from it, startled, and underneath the table I saw the green eyes and ragged fur of my friend. I crawled under the table, and he showed me how we could climb underneath the stage. It was a raised stage, built with metal struts holding it up. "I used to hide here as a child," he said.

"Luther, we'll die under here. We have to get out."

There was a panicked, trapped look in Luther's eyes. "I'll die out there, too. Better the flames than the hunter." He rolled over and showed me his side, where the fur was matted and slick with blood. "I can't run from him much longer." I looked out through the smoke and haze and saw Borut moving carefully through the sanctuary, hunting us.

Luther grunted and moved himself farther under the stage, pulling himself over the struts and supporting metal rods. "I'll be safer down here."

A booming voice called, "Luther. Come forth." We both turned, and on the far side of the stage his father was bent down, calling him. We both motioned for him to be silent, but he called again, louder. Luther made an exasperated sigh and crawled toward the end of the stage. I came close behind him. His father refused to come under the stage or to keep his voice down. Occasionally he would stand to look for Borut, then crouch back down and tell us to hurry.

When we pulled ourselves out, Reverend Martin said, "Luther, I've been blocking your way. You've used the church as an excuse not to come to Christ. You've used me as an example of why you shouldn't come to him. But your friends here, they are the church also, Luther. And they love you too. Your neighbor there, he is the church. And I'm sure there are others." He looked to me, and I nodded.

"The crazy scientist," I said. "That guy who thinks he's a robot, the half-zombie, Lara. They are the church, also. They're broken and ridiculous and possibly insane, but they love you, Luther. They are trying to help you find Christ in their own ridiculous ways. Surely you see that." There was a horrendous crashing sound as part of the roof collapsed and fell, leaving a burning trail before exploding in a shower of sparks on the floor nearby.

Luther turned from the spectacle of the disintegrating ceiling and spat onto the ground. "You keep talking about love, Father, but I've never seen it. I've never known that. The only person whose love I've never doubted is Clarissa, but she's seen enough of me at last and has taken Renata and moved out. This God you say loves me . . . how can that be? I am wicked and depraved. I have beaten my wife, Father, did she tell you that? I am so far below your Christ, why would he ever bother to notice me? And you say that he loves me. You say he would sacrifice himself for me, that he would die so I could live. Why? Why would he?"

A deep calm seemed to settle on Reverend Martin, and he took hold of Luther's forearms and said, "My son. When someone says he loves you, you need not always ask why. Sometimes it is enough to know that he does."

Luther tore his arms away from his father. "What do you know? My whole life you've hated me for what I am. You called that hunter here to kill me. Nothing would make you happier than to see me dead."

Reverend Martin gave a frustrated shout. "You always

misunderstand, Luther. I called the hunter because he was coming for you anyway, and I thought I might be able to help. I thought if you saw that death was coming for you, you might choose to cross the line from death into life."

"You don't understand what it's like, Father—"

He interrupted his son with a furious intensity, grabbing him by the arms. "I do understand!" Luther pulled away from him, his hands pushing against the wound in his side. The reverend looked up at his son and waited until Luther's eyes met his own. "The werewolf pelt over my desk is mine, Luther." He hung his head and turned slightly away from us. "It's mine because I was a werewolf once too. I've never been ashamed of you, Luther. I've been ashamed of myself for not knowing how to help. I don't know why, but it's always most difficult with your own family." He looked over his shoulder. "But I'll do what I can." He looked at me and said, "Get Luther out of here. I'll take care of Borut."

As he turned to go, a small dark shadow leapt up from behind a burning pew, a crossbow in his hand. "Death to the verevolf!" he shouted, and a silver bolt shot out at us like lightning. With an anguished cry, the reverend pushed Luther aside, and the bolt sank deep into the reverend's chest. He fell to the side, and Luther cried out and lowered him carefully to the ground. "Reverend? Can you hear me? Father?" His ears flicked forward, and he looked to me and said, "He's still breathing." He put his clawed hand lightly on his father's face. "Dad?"

The heat was unbearable now, and we felt our skin

starting to blister. The air was getting harder to pull into our lungs. I heard a cracking and popping from the ceiling and saw that the great beams that arced overhead like ribs were starting to give way. Borut had another bolt set into his crossbow and was preparing to fire. A piece of ceiling fell and knocked him off balance, and a shower of sparks burst up from behind the pew. We waited for Borut to leap back up, but he didn't, and Luther quickly pulled his father over his shoulder and shouted at me to follow. We ran as fast as we were able, Luther apparently ignoring the wound in his side, and moved up the aisle toward the sanctuary's exit.

Then Luther stopped and turned back toward the burning sanctuary.

"Luther, what are you doing? We have to get out of here."

He held up one clawed hand and waved me to silence, and his ears pricked up. "Someone called my name."

Luther pointed into the hottest part of the flames. "There is a man in there, consumed in flames. He's telling me to follow him deeper into the fire." Luther stared into the flames, and the smell of burnt fur and singed flesh mingled with that of charred wood and cloth.

Luther's eyes narrowed. "I can't see his face. Could it be the Clockwork Jesus? How did it get here?"

I looked and saw only flame, and the glowing certainty of things being burnt to ash in the furnace . . . pews, hymnals, flags, and pulpits little more than kindling. "Luther, there's no one there. We have to keep going."

But Luther was already lowering his father to the ground. "Get him to a hospital."

The roof creaked above us. "You're going to die if you go into those flames, Luther." I coughed. "We have to get out of here now."

Luther took one last look at his father and then bounded into the flames. I shouted for him to come back, but with a resounding finality a ceiling beam crashed to the floor, embers and burning pieces of ceiling showering me with sparks. Through the heat-twisted air I could just see Luther standing upright in the bonfire, as if speaking to someone, and then he was obscured by smoke and flame.

I staggered and dragged the reverend out of the church into the cool, clear air. I fell to the ground, and hands pulled us beyond the blistering heat of the church. They put the reverend on a gurney, and EMTs set to work, while the secretary hovered nearby and they wrapped me in a blanket. Fire trucks screamed into the parking lot just as the church, with a massive exhalation, collapsed into itself and fell flat.

THE WEREWOLF AND THE MOLTEN MAN

I thought I cared nothing for my father until I saw the bolt sticking from his chest like a tiny silver bone. Setting aside biological imperatives and Darwinian child-preservation explanations, I knew at once that he had done it because he loved me. Why he should love me I did not understand, but as the old man had said, sometimes it's enough merely to know. And I knew in that moment that there was no word in the English language sufficiently complex to explain my emotional attachment to my father. I hoisted him onto my shoulders, and Mikalatos and I made our way out of the sanctuary, the werewolf hunter under a pile of collapsed ceiling but still alive and my father laboring for each shallow breath.

As we moved out of the building, there came a voice from out of the heat and darkness, and it called my name. Startled, I looked to see who might know me in this place, and I saw a burning man. He told me to follow him, and I knew without question this was something I would do. I left my father and Matt without reservation and leapt into the flames. Behind me, the ceiling began to collapse. The pain in my side grew worse, and I put my hand to the sticky mess left by Borut's knife. I turned back, suddenly wishing I could go to the ambulance first and follow him later. But the posts from the ceiling blocked my path. I turned back to the burning man. He was wearing a long, white robe, and in the fire the white was as bright as a flash of lightning. He wore a golden sash, gold like the flickering tongues of the flames around us. His head and his hair were white, whiter than bleached clothing, whiter than cotton or snow or bone. His skin looked like metal glowing in a furnace, and his eyes—his eyes burned like the church was burning.

Weakened by the wound in my side, and certain at last that I had chased a hallucination into the flames, I lay down at his feet. And he said to me, "Don't be afraid. I am the first and the last. I died. But look, I am alive forever and ever, and in my hands are the keys to the grave and death." I looked up into his burning eyes and realized that if I died here, it wouldn't matter. If he truly held the keys to the grave, who is to say he could not bring me back from the dead? But I felt weak and frightened. He reached down, and his hands burned where they touched me and I could smell my fur lighting beneath his fingers. I patted out the flames, and through the smoke I saw Borut coming toward us, his crossbow in his hands.

"The volf is mine," he cried.

The burning man looked at him and nodded. Then he looked to me and asked, "Do you believe?"

Did I believe? That was his question? After all of this. I looked at him and shouted over the crackling flames, "It's too easy! After all these years, all this searching, you're going to bring it back to this question again? It can't be that easy. I do believe!"

Borut spit at my feet. "The devil believes. That is not enough."

I knew this was true. He was saying what I would have said in his place. "Is it enough to believe in you?" I grabbed hold of the man's burning feet and begged him to tell me this was enough. He lifted my chin toward his face.

"Come, follow me."

"I want to follow you. You must know that. But what is the cost?"

"If you wanted to build a house, Luther, would you start by counting your money to make sure you had enough? Do you have enough to finish this house if you start it?"

"I don't know. How much will it cost me to follow you?"

"If you were at war with a foreign king with an army twice as large as yours, Luther, an army you knew you could not defeat, what concessions would you make for peace?"

I looked to the floor. "I would give him whatever terms he asked for."

"In the same way, you must give up everything you have or you cannot be my follower."

Everything. My wife and daughter. My money, all of it. My house, my car, my television, my internet, my friends. My preferences, my rights, my comfort. A sudden regret seized me for many things I had done in life. I could not deserve life. The way I had treated my wife. Or my father, or my daughter, or my neighbors. These things would not be acceptable any longer. They were less than what was demanded of this King's servants. Less than would be demanded of a member of the royal family. I resolved to do away with those things, to give them to him if he desired them.

I knew enough theology to know that what he desired from me was everything. Not a life of some vague Christian veneer but a dedication to be his servant and his son. To follow his directions without question, to give myself to him fully, and perhaps at the end, when I had done everything he told me to do, I might hear him say, "Well done, good and faithful servant." And I would reply, "I am an unworthy servant, I have only done what you asked." I have only done what I said I would do in this moment, when I promised you everything in exchange for life. No excuses. Not living my life as if nothing has changed, not living like the people around me or settling into a comfortable life of moral superiority, but grabbing hold of my new identity as his servant with both hands and living a life of obedience to him that shows my allegiance is not to politics or government or a nation but to a Kingdom so far beyond those things as to make them less than a shadow. My allegiance is to a Kingdom that is growing and resolving itself in our midst, not through laws but through the transformation of human beings, by the change in human hearts.

I took his hand in mine and kneeled before him, and I kissed his hand. "I am your servant," I said. "May it be unto me as you have said."

He lifted me up and breathed into my face, and his breath burned as it entered my lungs, like a fire in my chest. I felt a searing pain on my forehead and right hand, and when I looked down I saw a scar growing on my hand, and it burned like scalding water.

"I demand his death!" Borut screamed. "He is a volf and belongs to me! This is the ending that must come for every monster!"

The burning man looked at him and said calmly, "Unless a seed fall to the ground and die, it cannot live."

He took hold of my snout and forced his fingers between my teeth, and with a terrifying speed and surprising strength, he yanked my jaw open, then pushed it farther until I felt my jaw begin to crack. I tried to shout, to tell him to stop, but he kept going until my jaw snapped like old firewood. I collapsed under his hands, sobbing, and he pulled my werewolf lips back and tore them. And he was not finished. I felt a hand in my side where the knife had wounded me, and then the excruciating pain of the tearing there, and I whimpered and closed my eyes. A last momentary regret washed over me as I realized that the burning man was killing me, and I was powerless to stop him. But it was, after all, what I had agreed to. Let him do as he will. I let my body go limp and felt my mind wander and then go free. And then only the heat and the flames and the dark.

205

CHAPTER 24

LAWN OF THE DEAD

THE FIREFIGHTERS POURED water onto the wreckage of the
church until it was little more than grey smoke and ashes.
I had screamed when it collapsed and shouted that there
were men in the building. The firefighters were combing
through the ashes now, and one of them found something,
grabbed it with a gloved hand, and yanked it out from under
a fallen beam. It was a wolf pelt, burnt and abused, with a
bloody hole torn down the center. It wasn't the reverend's
pelt. I could see that almost at once. And when the firefighters laid out the burnt thing, I could see the fresh skin
on the underside and a still-attached broken jaw on the head.
I sat down beside it, suddenly without the strength to stand.

I rolled up the pelt and tucked it under my arm. I couldn't believe he was dead. His father was already in the ambulance and had been taken away. I guessed I would have to take this to Luther's father, one final reminder of his boy. A sodden, torn, singed, and disgusting mess, but all that was left of him.

There was some commotion over by the church, and I walked through the crowd of neighbors and gawkers to see what it was. They had found a body. They pulled it out, broken and badly burnt, but I knew immediately by the size and the easy way they carried it that they had found Borut. They put him on a stretcher and immediately covered his face. I shook my head. It was the end that Borut expected, I'm sure, but it seemed like a waste.

I shifted the blanket on my back and huddled into it against the cold. There was another cry from the wreckage, and this time I struggled toward the front of the crowd for a closer look. A child shouted that someone was alive, and when I got close enough I saw that the firefighters were gathered around a pile of smoking refuse, and there was a thin hand protruding from it. The firefighters were examining it closely, and finally one of them pointed at a beam sticking up from the mess. Two of them pushed against it while a third reached down and quickly moved smaller bits out of the way, then reached his hand in the hole and pulled out a thin, naked man. He knelt, trying to cover himself and shaking in the cold, and I ran forward and threw my blanket around Luther's shoulders.

"You're alive," I said, and he smiled as if he was immensely grateful for those words, and then he lay down and slept.

I picked him up from the hospital a few hours later. Hibbs and Culbetron came with me, Culbetron because "I'm a doctor!" and Hibbs "Not because he's my friend or something human like that." Luther had been given a clean bill of health. After they'd cleaned him up, it had been discovered that there wasn't even a cut on him, and there was no damage from smoke inhalation or even burns. There was, Luther said, a strange new scar that ran from underneath his chin down to his stomach. It was thin and seemed to glisten in the light, and the doctor said it looked like a surgical incision from many years ago. When Luther said he didn't remember anything like that, the doctor looked at him skeptically and gave him a brochure about trauma and memory loss.

Luther didn't want to see his father, not yet, but he sent me in to check on him and I was assured all was well. The bolt had missed causing permanent damage, and the doctor thought a day or two in the hospital would be enough to make sure he was well, that there were no infections. Then we could get him back home. This relieved Luther, but he seemed reluctant to pay a visit. After some debate I gave Luther back his wolf pelt, which he took solemnly without a word.

We dropped Luther off at home, and I said good-bye to Hibbs and Culbetron. As I walked up to my house, I was surprised to hear the friendly neighborhood sound of someone mowing the lawn, which was strange given the time of year and the weather. I peeked over my fence and was amazed to discover that my yard was crawling with zombie gardeners.

They were clipping and mowing and fertilizing and moaning and shambling all over the place.

"That's it," I said. "I've taken all I can take, and I can't take no more." I snuck into the garage to get a chain saw, but we don't have a chain saw. The zombies had already taken out the lawn mower, the clippers, the hoe, and the rakes. The kids' baseball bat was missing. The only suitable weapon I could find was a broom. It would have to do. I held it over my head, and with a savage war cry I ran around the front of the house, kicked open the gate, and smacked the first zombie I saw right in the head with the bristly end of the broom. His head snapped backward, but then he stood up straight again and said, "You're home!"

"Of course I'm home. And now . . . it's clobbering time!" I took another swing and hit him in the head again. The zombie shook it off and looked over at the rest of the zombies.

"He's home," he said.

The other zombies turned toward me, and I took another swing at the zombie in front of me, who took the blow in good grace and said, "Master, we only want to serve you."

The zombies came closer, and I brandished my broom like a sword. "I'm not afraid to use this. Ask that zombie." I pointed at the one I had hit three times.

"It's true," he said. "He hit me three times."

Then they flooded over me in a big knot, as zombies are wont to do, and I tried to get out of it. I punched a zombie as hard as I could in the face. "My knuckles!" I shouted. Punching zombies hurt. I thought of all the zombie movies with heroes who end up somewhere with a big cache of rifles and found myself suddenly wishing I lived in the South.

"Remember the Golden Rule," one of the zombies said, and all of a sudden they were all taking turns punching me in the face.

"I don't think that's what the Golden Rule means," I managed to say between punches. Then one of them told me to turn the other cheek, and I did because I didn't have a choice, since they were holding me down. The last thing I saw was Robert running into the backyard, yelling at the zombies to stop.

CHAPTER 25

THE SYMPHONY
OF THE MAD SCIENTIST

AFTER MY BEATING AT the hands of the zombies, I woke up on Lara's couch, with Robert sitting across from me and Lara just walking in with a glass of water. I put my head back, almost too tired to care. "Please don't eat me. Or suck my blood. Or anything like that. I'm too tired to join the ranks of the undead."

"I'm sorry, Master," Robert said. "I told the other zombies what a great master you are, and they left Bokor. They're your followers now. See?" He opened the blinds and outside stood a ragtag group of zombies, pressed against the glass.

"Yay!" they shouted. Robert closed the blinds. They groaned.

"It took a while to convince them you were a mad scientist. But I eventually got through to them."

I bolted straight up. "I'm not a mad scientist, Robert, for crying out loud. I'm not a monster at all."

Lara handed me the water. She smiled at me gently. "You have all the classic signs, Matt. You think you're smarter than other people. You have your little knot of henchmen. You're trying to fix the world around you whatever the cost, never thinking of the damage you're doing." She gestured to the damage still in evidence from the fight with Borut in her living room. "You even have monsters following you and doing your bidding."

"No way. Robert is free now! He's not my zombie."

Lara sighed. "Show him your Bible, Robert." Robert pulled out his Bible.

"You see?" Lara gestured at the Bible. "It's small and covered in blue faux leather."

"I think blue leather is automatically faux. You're being redundant."

"Nevertheless, it's an NIV with a small flap, and on the flap are the letters MM."

I laughed. "That's not his Bible, that's my Bible."

"No," Robert said. "I got one just like yours. I want to be just like you. I met a girl named Krista last week and asked her out on a date. We're going to be married and buy the house next door to you."

"What? Robert, why does your Bible say MM on it?"

"Because yours does."

"Mine says MM because those are my initials."

"Oh."

"Good grief, Robert, I've told you a hundred times, don't be a zombie. Think for yourself."

"Sorry, Master."

I rubbed my face with my hands. "That still doesn't make me a mad scientist, Lara. I mean, Robert is a little dumb, you know. It's not my fault he thinks I'm his master."

Lara walked across the living room and came back with her mirror. She looked into it herself for a long time, and then with a melancholy sigh she handed it to me. "Look into this and tell me that you aren't a mad scientist."

I frowned, then held up the mirror. I wasn't sure I wanted to look. I was reminded of what Lara had said, that vampires could see themselves in the mirror, they just didn't want to see themselves any longer. I lifted it and held it out at arm's length.

I looked tired. My eyes had dark circles under them, and my hair stood up in every crazy direction it could go. It was hard to deny that there might be a slightly insane glint in my eyes. And Lara was right. I had a posse of henchmen (they might not like the description, but they did everything I told them to do), I had elaborate plans to fix the world around me, and frankly, I thought a lot of other people were idiots.

Lara said, "Also, you've been neglecting your family for your work. Now we just need a thunderstorm and a lightning rod attached to a corpse in your basement, and we have the beginnings of an excellent story."

She was right. I was neglecting my family. I pulled out my cell phone. Five missed calls from my wife. I looked again in the mirror and could see that I was wearing a white lab coat. Startled, I looked down and saw that I was actually wearing one.

"Where did this lab coat come from?"

Robert cleared his throat. "The other zombies took the liberty of dressing you."

I set the mirror aside. Robert was chewing on his thumbnail and watching me closely. I could see that he must be frightened, that he just wanted someone to give him answers, to give him certainty. "Robert, I know this is all well intentioned. But zombies . . . they're like an entire race of people who think they are following Jesus but are actually following a moral system . . . a list of what should and should not be done. And instead of knowing Jesus, instead of introducing people to Jesus, they're exporting a morality onto people who aren't able to follow that moral code . . . people who aren't in relationship with Jesus and don't have the help of the Holy Spirit.

"You're looking for some spectacular spiritual leader to give you answers to every hard question, instead of doing the hard work of finding out what God says about it yourself. People like Bokor are glad to give you an opinion about abortion and gay marriage and politics, and maybe they're still figuring out what to tell you about illegal immigrants. And I'm not saying those things don't matter, they do. But the Bokors of the world are so focused on those things, they're not doing something as simple as teaching you to live a life that would reflect the Sermon on the Mount. Your actions are divorced from anything about true faith."

Robert listened carefully, and with real pleading in his voice he said, "Bokor always showed us how the Bible says, 'A person is considered righteous by what they do and not by faith alone.' James 2:24." He pushed his Bible into my hands, and he was right. There it was, in black and white. Faith is not enough to justify us. Actions matter.

I read the whole chapter, trying to get the context, trying to find some clear clue that would show Robert the meaning, and I came across verse 14, which says, "What good is it, my brothers and sisters, if someone claims to have faith but has no deeds? Can such faith save them?" and it suddenly hit me that our churches are full of these people. Faith with no deeds. We believe in Jesus, we go to church, we lead semi-decent lives, but we aren't being transformed. We aren't changing. We don't think the deeds matter, because we have the "fire insurance." We're going to get into Heaven just fine, so we can keep lying and stealing and sleeping around and murdering and being selfish and whatever else it is we're doing.

But what James seemed to be saying was that a faith like that was a problem. It's not the deeds or lack of deeds that's a problem, it's that something is wrong with our faith if it's not producing actions. It's ineffectual. It's the sort of faith that fills a pew but leads us to a moment when we are face-to-face with Jesus and show him our works and he says, "I never knew you. Away from me, you evildoers!"

Robert shook his head. "You hate all of us zombies because we're a bunch of mindless slaves."

"I don't hate you, Robert, or the zombies. I don't even think they're all zombies. They look the same, but some of them are zombies wearing makeup to look alive, and some of them are humans wearing makeup to look like zombies. You can't tell them apart easily. Maybe the people will rise up and overcome the zombies eventually. Maybe a church like Bokor's can still become a living, vibrant place that will make a difference in the world. Maybe they'll be the sort of church that says, 'May your will be done on earth just like it is in Heaven,' and they'll really work to see that, to see earth become a place like Heaven."

I walked to the window and opened the blinds again. Lara winced and looked away from the sunlight. I stood there for a long time, overcome by my helplessness. I didn't know how to conquer a giant horde of zombies. There weren't enough chain saws and flamethrowers and brooms and grenades in the world. I could sit them down one by one and argue with them, or write a book, or try to shake them out of it and say, "Are you really following Jesus?" But in the end it would require God himself to do something, to open their eyes and make them see, just like I saw myself in the mirror. I dropped my head and, defeated, I prayed, "Dear Jesus, please fill Bokor's church and all the churches like it with your followers. Clear out the zombies, and fill our houses of half-life with your overflowing life." I thought of all the people who didn't know Jesus who thought that churches like Bokor's were a picture of what it meant to be a follower of Christ, and I shuddered.

I turned to see that Robert was crying, and Lara had put her hand on top of his. I put my hand on his shoulder. "Listen, Robert, don't lose hope."

Lara looked up at me, and there were tears in her eyes too. "Is there hope for people like us, Matt?" Just over her shoulder I saw the pile of stakes I had noticed earlier. I remembered how she had told me that sometimes dead was easier than undead, and I walked over and picked up one of them. I saw her eyes light up, though she tried to hide it, and she sat up taller when I walked back to her, testing the sharpness of the stake on my finger.

"Lara. Can I do whatever I want with these stakes?"

She closed her eyes and tightened her grip on Robert's hand. "Yes, Matt. I want you to. They're yours to do with as you please."

Robert's mouth tightened. "What are you going to do?"

I told him to be quiet. "Before I do this, Lara, I want to tell you something." She nodded but didn't open her eyes. "We know all about depravity, right? We've known our whole lives that we want to do wrong things, and we want to do them all the time. We talk all the time about how sinful we are, how evil. And I believe that to be true. At least, for me, I know it's true."

"It's true," she said. "It's true of me."

"But you know what we never talk about? We're made in

219

the image of God. That's what the Bible says. We were made in his image . . . a reflection of him."

Her eyes opened. "But then we fell from grace. In the Garden."

"Right. And then, when Adam and Eve had children, it says that they also were in the image of God. And God reminds Noah that human beings are made in his image. Which means that whatever happened in that moment—when human beings became sinful, or depraved, or whatever happened there—they never lost, somehow, being in the image of God. Which means that even at our worst, there's some piece of us that still reflects his image."

Robert shook his head. "No, we're totally depraved. If we're a reflection or representation of him, that would have to mean that God is completely depraved."

"I don't think so. It might mean that we've misunderstood what it means to be sinful. Or that we've emphasized it so much that we've simply lost sight of the fact that in our deepest, most horrific actions, some piece of us is still outside of that, some part of us is made in God's image, and that's not something we can ever completely eradicate. Or maybe God images himself through us despite our brokenness. I'm not sure how it works, but I do know that as we follow Jesus and become more like him, God is restoring his image in us. Like polishing a mirror or repairing a broken statue, he's changing who we are to more accurately reflect who he is. And no matter how dirty or broken or tarnished the mirror, he can eventually clean and repair and polish us until we shine like stars. There's hope for even the most monstrous among us."

Robert's eyes lingered on the stake I held in my hand, and his eyes darted to Lara and back to me. "So . . . what are you going to do with that stake?" Lara bit her lip and looked at me. I couldn't tell what she wanted anymore, though I had already decided what I would do. The stake was sharp, and I knew it could drive into her heart quickly and easily, whether it was by her hand or mine.

My phone rang, and I checked and saw that it was Krista. I quieted the ringer and slipped it back in my pocket. "I have to go in a minute. Robert, Lara, listen to this. Once Krista and I went to the Sydney Opera House in Australia. We sat where the choir would usually sit, so we could see every look on the conductor's face as he led this orchestra through Beethoven's *Piano Concerto no. 1 in C Major, op. 15*, Haydn's *Symphony no. 67 in F Major*, and Bartok's *Music for Strings, Percussion and Celesta*.

"At one point someone crinkled some paper on the other side of the auditorium, and the conductor gave them a practiced look of such insane anger that I think the person's bit of paper spontaneously combusted, and the ushers silently removed the offender.

"But then, during the break between the opening movement and the 'Largo,' someone started to applaud, and a short but well-intentioned outbreak of appreciation came from the audience. The conductor put his palms together and bowed with this slight smile on his face as if to say, *Ah, thank you for this applause. We are not finished yet, but I can see that our simple music has moved you. I can tell you have no idea of the true beauty of this third and longest cadenza we just played, and I imagine you will have no idea what to do at the end of our Bartok, when the chromatic theme is adapted to a diatonic environment. But for now you are impressed and perhaps truly appreciative so far as you are able, and you understand perhaps for the first time what it means when the Bard says that sheep guts can bring forth men's souls. So we accept your applause, though we are not yet finished. As for the paper crinkling and the coughing and that man there in the red shirt who keeps creaking about in his chair—these things I forgive you, because I see they were done in ignorance. And now, if you are quite finished, we will continue.*

"After that, the music filled the whole heart of the concert hall with a tapestry of beauty like I had never heard before. When the evening was over and the conductor returned continually to the front of the stage to receive still more applause, when our hands were raw and tired from playing a sort of music back to him and his orchestra, when he returned one too many times to the apron of the stage and bowed and smiled his superior smile, we forgave him, too, because what he had accomplished was not only some simultaneous reading of music but rather an organized reminder that we, yes, all of us, are made in the image of God. A man can take what is in his mind and scratch it out on paper, and others can fashion instruments, and still others sacrifice their lives to learn to bring pleasing sounds from these instruments.

For two hours we remembered that we human beings can provide the faintest echo of the words 'Let there be' spoken many millennia ago.

"Then we took the train back to our hotel, happy and tired and occasionally catching the eye of someone else in a collared shirt or an evening gown, and we were reminded that the stranger across the dirty train car and the conductor in his dressing room and the orchestra lugging home their instruments and maybe even ourselves . . . that there are moments when God reveals his likeness in the people around us. For those two hours we remembered that we need not be captives to our base selves, because by God's grace there stirs a deeper desire to be like the one who made us."

I took a deep breath and looked at them. Lara's eyes were closed again, and a smile had curled up at the edges of her lips, Robert's arm wrapped protectively around her shoulder. I scooped up every stake I could find in the house and quietly let myself out, crossed the street, and dumped them all into the trash.

CHAPTER 26

NO LONGER
MARRIED TO A WEREWOLF

As I DUMPED THE stakes into the trash, Krista threw open the door, her overnight bag slung over her shoulder and the kids in tow.

"Hey, Krista, where are you headed?"

She smiled at me patiently, but it was one of those smiles where the teeth didn't move when she said, "I'm taking myself to the hospital because someone won't answer his cell phone this week and my water just broke."

I had this brilliant insight that Krista wouldn't care what I had been doing or how great it was, so I gave her a quick hug, shoveled the kids in the back, and leapt into the van, and we were off to the hospital! That's why I heard this part of the story later, because it happened while we were at the hospital, when Krista was delivering our beautiful little girl. But here's how Luther told it to me.

Luther, ecstatic about his new state, called Clarissa as soon as he felt recovered from his experience in the church. He was bursting to tell her about his miraculous experience and so excited to spend an hour with her explaining that all would be better now, that he knew Christ, that they could go to church together and she and Renata could move back into the house. He couldn't wait to tell her that she was no longer married to a werewolf. She agreed to meet him once more, though she seemed reluctant on the phone, and this time Luther carefully avoided mentioning that she should bring Renata.

He cleaned the house from top to bottom, cleaned it so it shined, and even without his wolf nose he had to open all the windows to let some of the bleach and cleaning-solution fumes out of the house. He prepared the outside as well as he could and even took a day off work in anticipation of her visit. He got his hair cut and shaved himself carefully a half hour before her arrival. He bought flowers and put on his best suit, one she had bought for him, and he waited impatiently in the living room, in his easy chair.

When the doorbell rang he did his best not to run to the door. He threw it open, and before she could say a word he wrapped her up in his arms and held her tight. He was disappointed that her hug in return seemed cold, even businesslike, but she did say with what seemed genuine emotion, "I'm sorry about your father, Luther."

The reverend was doing well, actually, and Luther had even spoken to him once on the phone. He had tried to explain to his father that he wanted to be baptized, though it seemed like a strange and outdated ritual. He wanted to be submerged in the water, not sprinkled. He tried to explain this to his father, that it wasn't an issue with the Lutheran way, it was simply a passionate, burning desire to get as much of the consecrated water of the sacrament onto himself as possible. He couldn't explain it well, or felt that he couldn't. His father, with a mix of astonishment and delight, had assured him that he couldn't care less about the mode of the baptism and would be honored to attend when he was recovered. In fact, he reminded him, Martin Luther himself came down on the side of immersion in his Small Catechism, and it was perfectly acceptable as an adult to be immersed. Just before hanging up the phone, Luther blurted out that he would like his father to perform the baptism and then slammed down the phone, heart pounding and wondering if that was really true.

But now Luther was standing in the doorway of his house, his wife in his arms. He released Clarissa from his embrace and thanked her, and invited her into the house. She told him, again sincerely, that the house looked wonderful. "These are for you," he said, and showed her the flowers on the counter. Lilacs, her favorite. He hadn't bought them for her in some time.

Her lips creased in that certain way where the lines on the edges showed most clearly, the way they creased when she

NIGHT OF THE LIVING DEAD CHRISTIAN

was angry but trying to hide it. He wanted to ask her what was wrong, but more than that he wanted her to hear what had happened.

He started by saying, "Things have changed for me, Clarissa," and then the story of the fire came pouring out of him and he told her everything, not holding anything back. He found that he was opening up in a way he had not opened up with her for many years, and he felt hope kindling that their marriage might not just be saved, but might be healthy and wonderful and fun again. He assured her he would go to counseling with her if she wanted, and that he knew this might take some time, and he was willing to wait and to work hard. Yet before he was quite finished the lines around her lips became even more pronounced, and she had her head in her hands and would not look him in the eye.

"What's wrong, Clarissa?"

Without a word she set an envelope on the table and slid it across to him. She still wouldn't look at him, and he picked it up and slipped out the papers. It took a minute for it to register. Divorce papers. He tried to think of what he should say. At last he stuttered, "But I've changed, Clarissa. I've really changed."

"For once I believe you, Luther. I do." She still wouldn't look him in the eye. "It's just that it's too late. After all these years, you've finally changed, but I have too, Luther. I can't stay with you."

Luther took a deep breath and put his hand out for hers, but she flinched and pulled it away. He pulled his hand back.

"Very well, Clarissa. I said I would wait. I can wait. We can work this out in time."

"Oh, Luther." She tried to say something, then shook her head. "We'll talk later, Luther. I'm glad you've changed. I really am. Don't doubt that."

"I'll call you," he said. "We'll work this out."

She took off her wedding ring and set it on the table. Luther was stunned. He stared at it in disbelief. "There's someone else, Luther."

"Someone else?" He echoed her without even thinking the words, without knowing what he was saying.

"No one you know," she said quickly. "But he's a good man. Renata loves him, and so do I." She took a quick, stuttering breath. "I wanted to tell you sooner, Luther, but . . ."

He picked up her wedding ring. "But you were afraid." He pressed the ring into her palm. "Don't leave that here, Clarissa, please. If I ever meant anything to you, don't leave that here. Throw it away, or sell it. Save it for Renata. But don't leave it here."

"I don't want to give you the wrong impression, that there's still a chance."

He folded her fingers over the ring, unable to say anything more. He held his hand over hers for a long time. He didn't want to let her hand go, now that it might be the last time his hand would touch hers. He never thought a time like that would come, and here it was, in his living room, today.

Their hands parted, and he walked her to the door. She

stopped and hugged him, this time with real warmth, and before she fled down the steps she said, "Good-bye, Luther."

He stood at the door and watched her leave, and even after her car was gone he stood there, the door open, staring out at the driveway. It was a long time before he noticed that her tears had soaked his shirt when he held her.

CHAPTER 27

THE SKIN WE FIND OURSELVES IN

SITTING WITH MY WIFE IN THE HOSPITAL, I was reminded of how Jesus said that coming into relationship with God is like being born. It starts out with you feeling warm and happy and maybe just a little bit cramped, but you've got plenty of food coming to you with not much work involved, and then something tells you it's time to go, that it's time for a change, and there's unexpected pushing and pressure and pain and maybe a knife and cold air and crying and slapping and someone is sucking gunk out of your lungs and you're suddenly expected to breathe on your own and eat and grow up, and the world has changed and you're not quite sure it's for the better.

It's beautiful and strange and unforgettable. That's how it was for us as parents, to hold that little one in our arms and say, "She's safe and beautiful and ours." And especially for her big sisters, who loved her the moment they saw those tiny hands, and for her grandparents, who started loving her long, long ago, when Krista and I were still children. We named her Myca, which means "Who is like the Lord?" The correct answer being "No one."

Jesus used the words *born again* only once, when he was talking to a guy named Nicodemus. Nicodemus was a smart guy, but he was confused by the whole thing and started asking (I'm sure somewhat sarcastically) how he was supposed to crawl back into his mom's womb. It all winds up into what is probably one of the most famous speeches in the Bible and well, really, one of the most famous speeches ever, I guess. Famous enough for people to reference it from the bleachers at baseball games. Clockwork Jesus had mentioned it to us, and it was the Scripture that we read at Luther's baptism a few weeks later. Here's part of it:

"Just as Moses lifted up the snake in the wilderness, so the Son of Man must be lifted up, that everyone who believes may have eternal life in him. For God so loved the world that he gave his one and only Son, that whoever believes in him shall not perish but have eternal life. For God did not send his Son into the world to condemn the world, but to save the world through him. Whoever believes in him is not condemned, but whoever does not believe stands condemned already because they have not believed in the name of God's one and only Son. This is the verdict: Light has come into the world, but people loved darkness instead of light because their deeds were evil. Everyone who does evil hates the light, and will not come into the light for fear that their deeds will be exposed. But whoever lives by the truth comes into the light, so that it may be seen plainly that what they have done has been done in the sight of God."

But being born isn't the end of something. It's not some static moment that defines your relationship forever. It's a beginning—a significant one, yes, a coming to life. But if you remain a baby forever, something is terribly wrong. Here I was, years later, standing in front of my box of souvenirs, making room for another one. My vampire teeth were in there, and my were-squirrel tail, and my mummy hand. I folded up the mad scientist's lab coat and put it in the box too. I'm still growing, still learning, and although something happened years ago and I crossed over some invisible line from death into life, I'm also still in the midst of being res- urrected. There's all this death in me that's being eaten up by life. And even though it seems slow sometimes, I hope there's enough life pouring into me that it's coming up over the edges and onto the people around me. I hope that's true. Being born again can be painful. Growing up again—well, that's painful too.

One night not long ago, I heard wailing coming from Luther's house, through the rain and the darkness. It sounded like the distressed cries of the newly born, and when I ran across the street, I found him huddled on the side of the house, his wolf skin tied onto him with twine. He was crying in the rain, saying that he wanted her back and he thought that everything would be wonderful when he was born again, but he was wrong. It's not all wonderful. It's worth it, but it's not wonderful. I took him inside and stripped him out of the wolf's skin. I put a blanket over him on the couch and turned up the heater, and I sat with him for much of the night.

Sometimes when little Myca is crying, I hold her in her room and look for the fur or the little fangs. I wonder what she will struggle with, what she will need to overcome, and I pray that just as God was gracious to give her to us once, that he will protect her and guide her and that one day he will bless her with being born a second time, in that glorious, painful, ecstatic, amazing second birth. We gave her two middle names. The first is Anne, which means grace, because she is God's gracious gift to us. And her other name is Hope.

CHAPTER 28

A WEREWOLF SHARES HIS EPILOGUE

My father calls it a sunrise service. We get up in the cold and the dark, and since there is no longer any building, we gather down by the river. Not everyone from his church comes, though there are a few, and my friends come too. I don't hesitate to call them friends any longer. Matt is there with his family, the children rubbing the sleep from their eyes, and he and his wife looking tired. But Krista is proudly holding their newborn in her arms. Culbetron is there with his wife, Rachel, and Hibbs with his wife, Jen, and their children. Lara is standing there among them, grinning, and Robert is standing next to her, closer than I would have expected. I am surprised to see that my wife has come. My ex-wife. She has brought Renata with her, and they stand a little apart from the others. I am thankful for this unexpected act of generosity and surprised by it, and for a moment it makes me angry, because I have to wrestle with what it means that her boyfriend is not here. I decide, at last, that it is one more token of remembrance for what we once were to each other, that she is sparing me the pain of seeing him today, and she is allowing my daughter to share this moment with me.

My father wades down from the riverbank, his white robes responding to the current, and he holds his hands out to me. I follow him into the water. When we spoke of this a few weeks ago, Matt explained to me that this ceremony, for him, is the equivalent of a wedding ceremony. I am committed to God already, but now we have this celebration, this time for me to publicly declare my vows and let those around us see what has happened between me and my love.

The water is cold, and I can feel it tugging me under, but my father's hand on my shoulder is strong. He says a few words about the two kingdoms, one of light and one of darkness, and of the age-old war between them, and how the true light is shining and cannot be overcome. Then he asks me if I have renounced the kingdom of darkness and all the deeds and shameful actions of my past, the devil and all his ways, and if I am willing to turn away from those things to be a part of the Kingdom of light. I think before I answer, because it reminds me of the burning man's words, of his encouragement to consider whether I have enough to build this house. I find that I do.

I look into the assembled people until I find her face, and I say, as if to her, "I am sorry for my past actions, for the harm I have caused to others and to myself, for my sin. I gladly turn from those to serve in the Kingdom of light." I see an understanding in Clarissa's eyes. I know it is not a sign that we will get back together or even a promise that we will share custody of Renata or that things will be right between us, but there is this moment where she sees that I am sincere, that I am really and truly healed, that I am not the man I used to be. The corners of her lips turn up in a smile. Just the corners of her lips, but it has been so long since I have seen her smile.

Emotions are washing over me like the water, and I steady myself with a hand on my father's back. He looks into my eyes and for the first time I see that I have it in me to forgive him. Somewhere in me, and, I hope, sometime soon. He smiles at me with genuine affection and says, "Do you believe in God the Father Almighty, Maker of Heaven and earth?" I find that I do, and I say so. He asks if I believe in Jesus, God's only Son, and I know that I do. He is my Master now, you see, and I say so. And he asks if I believe in the Holy Spirit, if I believe that Christ died and was buried and came back to life and sits now at the right hand of God, and he asks me if I believe that Jesus will return to judge us, if I believe that my sins can be forgiven. I answer yes. I have spent so long trying to discover the "how" of each of these things—"How can my sins be forgiven?"—that I missed all along that I needn't care too much about the how if I really can receive forgiveness itself, that I should grab on to it and hold on tight. In other words, I do not know all the answers yet. I have more questions that must be answered, more questions than anyone is comfortable with. But I trust that the answers will be found somehow, someday in this relationship with Jesus.

My father puts his arm around me and his hand on my face and says, "Because of your profession of faith in our Lord Jesus

Christ and in front of these witnesses, I baptize you in the name of the Father, and of the Son, and of the Holy Spirit." He lowers me into the water then, and in the darkness I remember this same moment in the church, when the burning man took hold of me and tore me to pieces and I died just as Jesus had died, when a small seed of life fell into me and began to grow into something more. And then I am coming up out of death and the air rushes into my lungs, and there are cheers and hugs and tears and I find I am laughing. My father begins to sing, "Praise God from whom all blessings flow, praise him all creatures here below, praise him above, ye heavenly host! Praise Father, Son, and Holy Ghost." We say a prayer, and my father reads to us from the book of 1 John about how we once preferred the darkness but now we walk in the light as he is in the light. As my father reads, we can sense the sun just behind Mount Hood about to flood over the city. We turn our faces toward it, all of us—werewolves and vampires, zombies and mad scientists—and eagerly wait for the sun to rise and make us human.

Acknowledgments

WRITING A BOOK REQUIRES a lot of parts to be stitched together before you can shoot it full of lightning and bring it to life. I am immensely thankful for the many people along the way who served as lackeys, fellow scientists, and resources for this book. First, to Dan and Rachel Culbertson and Peter and Jen Hibbs, who sat quietly and without complaining while I carved up their lives and characters for my own nefarious purposes. It was Dan's idea to clone Jesus from the Communion elements, and I am certain that the robotic overlords will be pleased with the performance of the Hibbs 3000. Thanks, guys.

To Marc Cortez, who helped me navigate the potential response of the people in the village below my castle. If I manage to avoid being skewered by pitchforks, I have Marc to thank. Even if he (inexplicably) thinks zombies are better than vampires.

To John Rozzelle, who took the savage excision of his character (Señor Muerte, the Mexican priest turned super-hero and *luchadore*) with exceptional grace and good humor,

241

just as you would expect from a religious superhero. Fret not, my friend. Señor Muerte will ride again on his flame-bedecked motorcycle! Evil beware!

To Greg Horton, the slayer of the mole men. The entire world is in your debt for your service. Thank you for your insightful words and for giving my work a second chance. This book is better for your input.

Adrian Rivero, the only member of the Hate Club to be accidentally dropped from the acknowledgments in the last book. Sorry, Riv. Don't kill me in your comic! Don't kill me in real life either.

To Ken and Sarah Cheung, who I left alone purely out of respect for your newlywed status. Congratulations!

Shasta Kramer, for playing Igor to my mad scientist. Thank you for bringing me meals and milkshakes, reading early drafts and the first complete manuscript, for being a great encouragement and for naming Borut! I appreciate you and your friendship a great deal.

Derek McLarty, who has the singular chore of being my real neighbor. I hope you don't mind that I stole a couple details from the neighborhood. And let it be known to all that Derek is the real King of Halloween who gives out full-sized candy bars. I appreciate your kindness to my kids and our family.

To Wes Yoder, Sarah Atkinson, and Brittany Buczynski, who processed enough revisions, reboots, restructures, rewrites, alternate timelines, character additions, deletions, and do-overs to stretch the limits of sanity. Remember the Halloween Angel? The MONSTER VISION! glasses? The Weird Magnet? I do.

I hope you remember them all as fondly as I do. I appreciate you and your hard work and friendship.

To Beth Sparkman, for leading the process on yet another fabulously designed book, and to Jen Ghionzoli, the designer, who I am told is owed a pizza by me, and also to Ruth Berg, who drew all the silhouettes and is, in fact, completely responsible for me learning to spell the word *silhouette* . . . great work. It looks amazing.

And to the rest of the Tyndale family . . . the world at large has no idea how instrumental each of you is in the making of so many books (this one included). I wish I could thank each of you personally, and I hope you know how much you are appreciated. THANK YOU for your continual encouragement, and for going above and beyond the call of duty for this book.

To Mom, Dad, Janet, and Terry, thanks for your support, advice, and for all the help with the kids!

To Zoey, Allie, and Myca. I love you all. Thank you for being such wonderful daughters.

And, of course, to Krista, who deserves far more thanks than can be wedged into an acknowledgments section. Thank you for your love, care, and generosity, and thank you for the hammock, which allows me to write in considerable comfort and style. I love you and am thankful for your friendship and support. Don't worry, your book is coming soon!

Lastly, to all my minions and friends at BHR, VBC, NCC, CIA, WSN and CCC. It is an honor to be a part of so many three-lettered secret societies. You are all my BFFs. For. Ev. Er. Whether you like it or not.

INTERVIEW WITH THE AUTHOR

Q. What is it with you and monsters? First a mob of imaginary Jesuses and a talking donkey, now werewolves and vampires?

A. I blame my father. Starting when I was a toddler, my dad would watch the Saturday morning *Monster Matinee* with me. The first movie I remember seeing was *Them!*, which was a movie about giant man-eating, irradiated ants. There's also a family legend about a time my dad was left alone with me, and I marked my hand with a green marker. He said I must be "turning into the Incredible Hulk," which induced nonstop wailing until my mom came home and washed my hands. From a young age, science fiction and fantasy movies, television, and books were part of my life. Not to mention comic books! That offbeat way of looking at the world is part of who I am.

Q. Where did you get the idea for this book? What made you think to use monsters in a spiritual, allegorical way?

A. Years ago I read a sociology book that pointed out that vampires are essentially twisted, perverted versions of the Christ story. Christ gave his own blood freely so that people he loved could live forever. Vampires steal blood from others to selfishly prolong their own lives. The symbolic power of monsters to represent frightening things about our own nature has always been part of the genre, whether you're reading *Frankenstein* or watching *Night of the Living Dead*. I hijacked that a bit by bringing a spiritual dimension to it and altering the mythology to better fit my purposes where necessary, but the basic seed of the idea really came from that sociology book and from wanting to find a unique way to talk about the search for personal transformation.

Q. In your first two books, you appear as a main character in the story. Where did you come up with this unusual literary device? Or is it just shameless narcissism?

A. It first popped into my head because Wes Yoder, my agent, and I were discussing an early draft of *Imaginary Jesus*, which was actually a series of humorous essays. Wes said it needed a stronger narrative, which got us talking about Dante's *Inferno*. You can actually see some strong similarities in structure between *Imaginary Jesus* and parts of the *Inferno* (author as narrator and main character, "guides" through the spiritual realms, strongly episodic events, "real" people appearing as characters). With *Night of the Living Dead Christian* I wanted to back off from that and make it less autobiographical, so I'm the narrator, but really the main character, the heart of the story, is Luther Martin. I suppose in my third book I'll just make a cameo appearance, and in the fourth there won't be any sign of me at all!

Q. Your writing style has been described as "C. S. Lewis meets Monty Python" or "a happy-go-lucky C. S. Lewis." What's your reaction to those comparisons?

A. First of all, it appears that people think I'm British! The reviews and comparisons are flattering, and I'll do my best to live up to them. I hope that what people are saying is, "Here are books about God that I enjoy reading." That's what I think of when I think about C. S. Lewis and what I'm trying to provide for my readers.

Q. You seem to enjoy meshing fictional characters with real-life situations and people (including yourself). Why do you write this way, rather than writing straight fiction?

A. In the midst of all the surreal and allegorical in my novels, writing about real-life situations and people keeps me grounded in reality. For instance, I try to make sure that my stories end like real life, not necessarily in the way I would want them to end. Which means that sometimes there are situations that aren't resolved, and endings may not be completely happy, even if they are hope-filled. Also, I like blurring the line between "fiction" and "reality" in a way that reminds us that the words *fiction* and *truth* are often complementary to one another—in other words, that we can use fiction as a tool to illuminate truth.

Q. If Clockwork Jesus were real, what one question would you ask him?

A. In one sense, since he's purely a recording of the words of Christ from Scripture, he does exist. The first question that comes to mind is why he continues to allow injustice in the world, which basically boils down to the question of the martyred saints in Revelation: "How long, O Lord, holy and true?" I am looking forward to his return and an end to the suffering and waiting of this life. Wow—that sounds like a downer in a comedy novel, but that's certainly the question in the forefront of my mind.

Q. In the book, you discuss how all people are made in the image of God, despite the evil things we do. Do you believe that even someone like Hitler was made in the image of God?

A. It's sort of an all-or-nothing question, isn't it? If God made humanity in his image, that would include Hitler as well as Mother Teresa, whether we like it or not. As we move closer to being like Christ, the image of God becomes clearer in us, so it stands to reason that it may become more distorted as we move away from Christ. Regardless, the worst human beings continue to have been created in God's image, and there is always hope that God can move them forward in the process of restoration.

Q. Is Borut the monster hunter based on a real person?

A. No way. And if I knew a guy like that, I wouldn't base any characters on him because he might shoot me with a crossbow.

Discussion Guide

1. As a child, what were you afraid of?

2. Luther quotes two famous philosophers: Seneca, who wrote *homo homini res sacra* ("man is something sacred to man"), and Plautus, who wrote *lupus est homo homini* ("man is a wolf to man"). Who do you agree with? Have you seen more people treating each other with care or with cruelty?

CHAPTERS 1–3

1. Were you surprised that Matt wanted to protect the werewolf after it attacked him? Have you ever felt compassion for someone without knowing much about that person's situation?

2. When Borut says his crossbow is "the only cure" for the werewolf, what do you think he means?

3. When the woman tells Matt that her husband is a "monster," what do you think she means?

4. The zombies that attack Matt and his friends aren't typical monster-movie zombies. How are they different? What do they want?

CHAPTERS 4–5

1. When Matt says, "We all have little mutations," what does he mean? Do you agree with him?

2. Do you know any Christians who celebrate Reformation Day instead of Halloween? What do you think about Christians celebrating or not celebrating Halloween?

INTERLUDE

1. Do you think guilt is a result of "cultural programming"? Why do people experience guilt, and what methods have we developed to cope with it? When you feel guilty, what do you do to resolve those feelings?

2. "None of us desire to remain wolves. All of us desire to remain wolves." What does this paradox mean? Do you think it's true?

CHAPTERS 6–7

1. Matt's neighbor explains his condition by saying, "I turn into a wolf when I'm angry." Are there aspects of your personality that appear when you get angry, depressed, or upset?

2. When Matt finds out his neighbor has read *Imaginary Jesus*, Matt assumes he wants to learn about being a Christian. Is that what Luther says he wants? If not, what is the difference?

3. Do you agree more with Matt's or Dr. Culbetron's definition of what it means to be a Christian? Is there more to Christianity than what a person believes? How does being "born again" figure into the equation?

4. Write your own definition of a Christian. How does it compare with Matt's and Dr. Culbetron's definitions?

INTERLUDE

1. Luther's father tells him, "Good theology domesticates our baser instincts." What does he mean by that? Do you think Luther's father is correct or misguided on this point? Why?

CHAPTERS 8–11

1. Do you identify more with Matt or with his wife, Krista? Do you find yourself saying, "I'll be home later," or are you the one asking, "How much later?" When you spend a lot of time away from your family on other activities, how do your parents/spouse/ children react?

2. Dr. Bokor says that real change "can be accomplished through hard work, discipline, and an unwavering commitment to the truth in this book," the *Dr. Bokor*

Study Bible. What do you believe people need to experience true change?

3. Do you think it's better for people to be exposed to danger so they can learn discernment or to simply trust their leaders and be sheltered from danger? Why?

4. Is it true that "Jesus wants [your] brain, not [your] heart"? Is the expression "ask Jesus into your heart" literal or just a figure of speech? How would you describe what happens at the moment of conversion?

INTERLUDE

1. Luther says, "I want payment now. I want to know that my life will be better today." Is there anything wrong with that desire? Does the Bible say anything about the rewards in this life for following Christ?

2. Do you agree that "belief gets us into Heaven regardless of behavior"? Is there biblical support for this idea? Is it true that "Satan's theology must surely be as informed as the most learned Christian scholars"? What bearing does this have on Satan's eternal destiny?

3. What's your reaction to the quote by Gandhi? Have you or people you've met ever felt similarly? How would you approach a conversation with someone who felt this way?

CHAPTERS 12–15

1. Lara says all monsters can be cured "if they want it
    badly enough." What do you think she means? Give
    an example of a disease or condition that requires the
    patient's cooperation in order to cure.

2. Lara describes the pain from Borut's crucifix as "some
    internal heater in my blood, and it was starting to
    boil." What do you think that means? Why do you
    think people have adopted the crucifix as a symbol
    of protection against vampires?

3. Explaining why vampires avoid mirrors, Lara says, "If
    you never see yourself the way that you really look, it's
    pretty easy to be satisfied with your life." Do you agree
    with that? What "mirrors" do you avoid looking into?

4. Lara says Borut will have to leave Luther alone if he
    overcomes his lycanthropy because "it's one of the
    rules." What rules is she referring to? Why does Borut
    want to kill Luther?

CHAPTERS 16–18

1. When Lara says Borut is "more a force of nature than a
    man," what do you think she means?

2. As "a vampire with a tan," Lara is a walking paradox,
    still fighting to overcome her thirst. Are there areas
    in your life that make you feel the same way? What
    behaviors and desires do you routinely struggle against?

3. Luther tries to follow Dr. van Pelt's instructions "to remain a werewolf but not behave as a werewolf." Why doesn't this work when Luther becomes angry? How is this behavioral modification technique different from the cure Lara offered?

4. What's your reaction to Matt's dream, described at the end of chapter 18?

INTERLUDE

1. "Is not love based in some way upon the excellent qualities of the object of our love?" Do you agree with this claim? What types of love do you think Luther is describing?

2. God's sending Jesus to earth to save humanity is compared to a man adopting ants as his own children. Is this an accurate analogy?

3. How would you answer someone who argued that "we must choose between no God or a loving one"?

CHAPTERS 19–21

1. Our culture frequently encourages us to accept ourselves as we are. As Luther says, "Shouldn't I embrace me and be at peace with who I am?" What do you think of this? Do you love yourself the way you are, or do you think you need to change?

2. When the Clockwork Jesus is asked for the answer to eternal life, are you surprised that he doesn't mention

faith or belief? How would you answer the question, "What must I do to be saved?"

3. Despite the answer from the Clockwork Jesus, Matt reasons that our actions alone can't save us if we don't believe Jesus is the Son of God. Then he asks, "But could our beliefs alone save us?" What do you think? Can they?

CHAPTERS 22–23

1. Reverend Martin says Luther can be cured of his lycanthropy and find salvation—"not only salvation in the sense of some future heavenly kingdom, but salvation today." What does he mean?

2. "When someone says he loves you, you need not always ask why. Sometimes it is enough to know that he does." Does this mean God's love for humans can't be explained, only accepted? How does this relate to salvation by faith?

3. What did you think about Luther's father sacrificing himself for his son? Would you take a bullet (or an arrow) for someone you love? How about for someone you hated? Who would take one for you?

INTERLUDE

1. How does Luther know his father loves him?

2. When the burning man asks Luther, "Do you believe?" why does Luther say belief is "too easy"? Do you agree with him?

3. How does belief being "too easy" relate to the burning man's requirement that Luther give up everything to follow him?

4. If someone asked you to give up everything, what would be the hardest thing to surrender? What would you want to hold back?

5. The burning man and Luther's father both say, "Unless a seed fall to the ground and die, it cannot live." This is a paraphrase of John 12:24, "Unless a kernel of wheat falls to the ground and dies, it remains only a single seed. But if it dies, it produces many seeds." Why is this message important enough to be repeated? How does it apply to Luther's struggle with lycanthropy?

CHAPTERS 24–26

1. What is the significance of Luther's new scar?

2. Have you ever been tempted to think of your faith as "fire insurance"? Why do our deeds still matter if faith is what saves us?

3. Describe your beliefs about the image of God in humanity. What does it mean to be "made in the image of God"? Do our evil actions remove that image or just tarnish it? Is it possible to restore it? How?

4. If you were in Clarissa's position, would you have done the same thing she did? If you were in

Luther's position, how would you have reacted to Clarissa's news?

CHAPTERS 27–28

1. How are newborn Christians like newborn babies?

2. When Matt folds up his mad scientist's lab coat and puts it in his trophy box, what is he really doing? What do you need to leave in your own trophy box?

3. Why does Luther tie his wolf skin back on?

4. How is a baptism ceremony like a wedding ceremony?

5. Like Luther, do you ever focus too much on the "how" of salvation, forgiveness, the Second Coming, etc., instead of just grabbing on to those things and holding tight? What questions would you most like to have answered? Do you feel it's okay to not know all the answers?

6. Read 1 John 1:5-7, the passage Luther's father reads at the end of the baptism. Why is following Jesus described as "walking in the light"? How can leaving the darkness and walking in the light "make us human"?

SUMMARY QUESTIONS

1. Why do children like to sleep with a night-light? Why does Jesus call himself "the light of the world" (John 8:12)?

2. Did this book challenge you or make you uncomfortable? What questions did it raise in your mind?

3. What was your favorite scene in the story? Go back and reread it. Then discuss why that moment resonated with you.

4. How would you explain the book's overall message or bottom line?

5. Read the "Are You a Monster?" guide in the back of the book. Which monsters sound familiar? Have you seen them in person? Do any of the monsters remind you of yourself?

ARE YOU A MONSTER?

A Layman's Self-Diagnosis Guide to Common Monstrosities

GARGANTUANS

OVERVIEW: Gargantuans are creatures that have grown to enormous size: an ape as large as a skyscraper, a lizard so huge it has to live in the ocean, a wolf as big as a house, etc. They tend to attract large crowds of curious seekers who want to see what the giant monsters will do next. Demanding, powerful, and hungry, one gargantuan can do more damage with a single flick of a tail than many other monsters combined.

COMMON HABITATS: Once fully grown, gargantuans require large venues, such as stadiums, large conferences, rock concerts, and megachurches.

WEAKNESSES: Honest feedback, becoming so big that "no one understands," feeling of invincibility or being above the law, temptation to crush "the little people" all around them

NATURAL ENEMIES: World War II biplanes, internet dissidents, other gargantuans, themselves, small women in red dresses, gravity

SYMPTOMS INCLUDE: Becoming "huge" sensations; thinking that just because everyone listens to them, they have something important to say; increasingly large picture of themselves; desire to eat an entire semi full of cookies

COMMON QUOTES: "I'm the biggest and the best!" "Behold my 170,000 followers on Twitter!"

If you think you or a loved one may be a monster, please visit
www.nightofthelivingdeadchristian.com for help and resources.

INVISIBLE PEOPLE

OVERVIEW: Invisible people are those who have perfected ways to avoid detection in everyday situations. As such, they are always skulking around, eavesdropping on private conversations, seeing things they have no business seeing, and then passing that information along to others. Invisible people can often be found working "behind the scenes" to manipulate others into doing what they want

COMMON HABITATS: Unknown—rarely sighted

WEAKNESSES: Getting drenched with buckets of paint; being followed or barked at by dogs; although they can't be seen, they do leave tracks; can rarely avoid bragging about their invisible exploits for long

NATURAL ENEMIES: People who refuse to "take their word for it" that they "heard it firsthand"; night-vision goggles; warm weather, when dressing in layers of clothing raises suspicions; other invisible people; the truth

SYMPTOMS INCLUDE: "Innocent" lingering near others' conversations, desire to hack other people's e-mail accounts, late-night Facebook stalking, obsession with knowing the latest gossip, tweaking what other people say to match their own agendas

COMMON QUOTES: "That's not how *I* heard it happened. What really happened was this . . ."

MAD SCIENTISTS

OVERVIEW: The mad scientist is an individual of above average intelligence (or so he will tell you) who has "the answer" to any problem he comes across. With great enthusiasm and greater arrogance, the mad scientist will build impressive plans and devices to "fix" the world around him—whether the world wants it or not.

COMMON HABITATS: Laboratories, castles, chemistry stores, corporate R & D departments, Mensa gatherings

WEAKNESSES: Overweening pride, inability to see another point of view

NATURAL ENEMIES: Peasants with pitchforks, monsters of their own creation, people in authority, self-awareness

SYMPTOMS INCLUDE: Megalomania; feeling misunderstood and underappreciated; gathering of syncophantic "minions" or "lackeys" whenever possible; wild, unkempt hair; lack of fashion sense; taking recreational IQ tests; pulling all-nighters in the lab; passionate desire to own the latest technology

COMMON QUOTES: "Here's what I would do if I were in charge. Mooowhahaaahaaaaaa!"

MUMMIES

OVERVIEW: The mummy is a king who died long ago but is still treated with the respect and honor of a living king. Typically wrapped in the finery and beauty of his past achievements, the mummy demands allegiance regardless of his present actions, making it difficult to see that what lies beneath is little more than putrified flesh.

COMMON HABITATS: Pyramids, long-established ministries and workplaces, pulpits, creepy tombs

WEAKNESSES: Getting trapped in tombs, occasionally being mistaken for toilet paper, excessive reliance on past achievements, overwhelming urge to curse anyone who disagrees with them

NATURAL ENEMIES: Healthy dissent, consensus decision making, Brendan Fraser, sandstorms, "new" people who look at the present rather than the past reality

SYMPTOMS INCLUDE: Grandiose verbiage; intense desire to wrap oneself in long, winding cloths; demand for unquestioning obedience; fear of change; insistence on "proper respect"; hoarding gold, jewels, and servants and putting a curse on them

COMMON QUOTES: "Perhaps you do not recall the glory of my empire in ages past!"

ROBOTS
(ANDROIDS, CYBORGS, ETC.)

OVERVIEW: Robots are beings with prodigious intelligence, often coupled with stunted emotions. They are swift problem solvers and possess inhuman strength. They have an unstoppable focus on objectives rather than people and are sometimes baffled by the illogical emphasis placed on the overwrought emotional responses of others

COMMON HABITATS: Starships, finance departments, the future

WEAKNESSES: Getting caught in the rain without an oil can, being disassembled by scavengers, inability to tell when they have hurt someone's feelings, lack of awareness of their own emotions, social awkwardness and/or relational immaturity

NATURAL ENEMIES: Rust, water, illogic, sentimentality, Dr. Phil

SYMPTOMS INCLUDE: Inability to speak using contractions, metallic sheen to the skin, preference to working with data over people, perpetual worry that their "charge will run down," often accused of being cold or aloof

COMMON QUOTES: "Thank you for informing me that you love me. I will carefully consider a proper response and get back to you in a period of no more than fourteen days."

sAsquATcHEs

OVERVIEW: The sasquatch or "forest ape" is a solitary creature who feels no need for the company of others. He is often seen from a great distance, loping across a field or eating a handful of berries. The more highly socialized sasquatch may occasionally make forays into the most anonymous social situations.

COMMON HABITATS: Isolated forests, MMORPGs, tree houses, internet churches, Wyoming

WEAKNESSES: Poorly suited to city life, sometimes forgets how to interact with others, hates being called a "Yeti," occasional stench from lack of bathing, may suffer from social anxiety

NATURAL ENEMIES: Zombies, potlucks, poison ivy, shaving cream

SYMPTOMS INCLUDE: Increased hairiness, inappropriate comments and behavior in social settings, bitter anger toward organizations of various kinds, using privacy as an excuse for reclusive habits, intense desire to watch *Harry and the Hendersons* (again)

COMMON QUOTES: "I need my space." "The church is too institutionalized. I'd rather go off alone, just me and God."

TRolls

OVERVIEW: Trolls are largely solitary creatures who haunt lonely places in search of more gold, riches, and food. They tend to take without asking, and they jealously guard their hoards, often with giant spiked clubs.

COMMON HABITATS: Mountain dwellings, under bridges, bank vaults, MBA programs

WEAKNESSES: Constant fear that someone will "take their stuff" causes them to be generally untrusting and untrustworthy; easily manipulated by appealing to their greed.

NATURAL ENEMIES: Billy goats, sunlight, thieves, invisible hobbits, vampires, the annual tithing sermon, visiting missionaries, slide shows of natural disasters that ask for money at the end

SYMPTOMS INCLUDE: Ravenous hunger; the "gold itch," paranoia, premature greying of the skin, unrelenting suspicion that "my things would be safer if I lived in a cave"

COMMON QUOTES: "Mine, mine, all mine!"

VAMPIRES

OVERVIEW: Vampires steal the life force of others to increase their own longevity, gladly using the lives and well-being of those around them to increase their own quality of life. As such, they are intensely selfish creatures with a strong sense of self-preservation. They are difficult to destroy and often capable of taking a variety of shapes to escape dangerous situations.

COMMON HABITATS: Coffins, Eastern European bloc countries, night clubs, caves, Goth concerts

WEAKNESSES: Afraid of sunlight, holy water, mirrors, and crucifixes; can't cross running water; can be killed with wooden stakes. As you might imagine, with so many weaknesses, they are big scaredy-cats.

NATURAL ENEMIES: Let's just say they don't often have many friends.

SYMPTOMS INCLUDE: Pale skin, avoidance of daylight and looking into

mirrors, habit of turning the conversations back to themselves, inability to form lasting relationships without eventually eating their friends
COMMON QUOTES: "I've gotten all I need from you."

wEREWOlvEs

OVERVIEW: A werewolf (also called a lycanthrope) is a human being who wrestles with animalistic, instinctual urges that occasionally grow difficult or impossible to control. Once the urge grows to a certain point, the werewolf changes from human to wolf form and gives himself over to the desires of his wolf self. This can be on a monthly cycle or far more often. Lycanthropy can be transmitted to others, typically through a deep bite from an infected person.

COMMON HABITATS: Werewolves are well adapted to urban environments, with recent outbreaks reported in Paris, London, and America. Werewolves can thrive in any habitat humans thrive in. They can also survive in the wilderness while in wolf form, assuming they have sufficient prey to hunt.

WEAKNESSES: Silver bullets, dog food, wolfsbane

NATURAL ENEMIES: Montana ranchers, lumberjacks, dog catchers

SYMPTOMS INCLUDE: Sudden hairiness; primitive, almost overwhelming urges that are difficult to control; howling at the full moon; eating chickens or other animals raw (fondness for sushi is common); anger or irritability; increased night vision

COMMON QUOTES: "Howwoooooooo!"

ZOMBIES

OVERVIEW: Zombies are people who appear to be alive, to have rational thought and volitional movement, but who have actually been infected with a deadly sickness that creates the illusion of life in dead creatures. Zombies have an insatiable hunger to make others into zombies just like them. This desire becomes the overriding motivation for everything the zombies do.

COMMON HABITATS: Churches, political movements, cults, riots, post-apocalyptic landscapes

WEAKNESSES: Lack of original thought, often unaware of undead state, slavish devotion to a "bokor" or master, require community with other zombies to receive constant assurance that "this is what it's like to be alive"

NATURAL ENEMIES: Chainsaws, situations that require climbing ladders, nonconformists, vultures

SYMPTOMS INCLUDE: Lockjaw; unquestioning obedience to a certain belief, leader, website, or author; stiffness of limbs; undead stench; appearance of life; greenish tint to skin; hunger to make others like themselves in every way

COMMON QUOTES: "Braaains! We want your braaaaaaains!"

REJECTED TITLES AND TAGLINES

SOMETIMES NAMING a book requires excruciating patience and the input of editors, salespeople, the author, and the public at large. Here are some titles we considered for *Night of the Living Dead Christian*. We considered some of them longer than others. Feel free to pick your favorite and write it on the front of the book with a marker.

Alternate Titles

> The Werewolf Who Went to Church
> Half Life
> The Monster Cure
> Fangs for the Memories
> Baptism by Werewolf
> Embracing Moonlight
> Monsters in the Mirror
> Matt Mikalatos and the Curious Case of the
>   Neighborhood Werewolf
> Late Afternoon of the Living Dead Christian
> Return of the Son of the Attack of the Living Dead
>   Christian, Part 3: The Sequel

Until Sunrise
Love Her or Luther
So I Married a Werewolf
A Portrait of the Werewolf as a Young Man
Werewolf Shrugged
To Catch a Wolf
I, Werewolf
The Monsters of Madison County
The Werewolf Always Rings Twice
When Hairy Met Sally
Confessions of a Lutheran Werewolf
The Wolfman Cometh
Jesus, the Wolfman, and Me

Alternate Subtitles

A Story of Faith, Fur, and Transformation
The Funniest Book about Spiritual Transformation
   You'll Read This Year
The Silly Side of Sanctification
Surrounded by Monsters, with Theology His
   Only Weapon
If We Have Anything to Say about It, They Won't
   Stay Dead
You'll Be Howling . . . with Laughter!
Sometimes You Have to Throw Your Neighbor a Bone
The Story of a Wolf in Man's Clothing

A LETTER FROM MATT MIKALATOS

Dear Reader,

After our harrowing experience together, no doubt you would like to share your thoughts with me, the author. Perhaps the easiest way to do this is via the disembodied communication device we call . . . THE INTERNET!

ENTER MY WEBSITE OR BLOG . . . IF YOU DARE!

www.mattmikalatos.com
www.mikalatos.blogspot.com

BEHOLD! AN ENTIRE WEBSITE MADE UP OF HUMAN FACES! OH, THE HORROR:

www.facebook.com/matt.mikalatos

FEEL THE PRESSURE OF SAYING SOMETHING IN 140 CHARACTERS OR LESS ON TWITTER:

@mattmikalatos

FIND A FREE, DOWNLOADABLE, AND NOT AT ALL SCARY VERSION OF THE BOOK DISCUSSION GUIDE:

www.bookclubhub.net

SUMMON ME TO SPEAK TO YOUR CHURCH, WRITER'S CONFERENCE, OR ORGANIZATION.

Ambassador Speakers Bureau
info@AmbassadorSpeakers.com
615-370-4700

And now, Gentle Reader, I bid you good night. Until the next time . . .

Fondly,

The Author

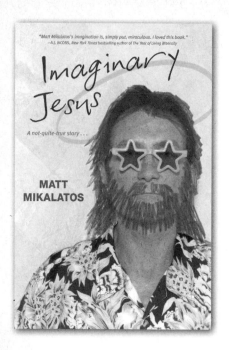

"Matt Mikalatos's imagination is, simply put, miraculous. I loved this book."
—A.J. JACOBS, *New York Times* bestselling author of *The Year of Living Biblically*

Imaginary Jesus

A not-quite-true story . . .

MATT MIKALATOS

Matt Mikalatos liked Jesus a lot. In fact, he couldn't believe how much they had in common. They shared the same likes, dislikes, beliefs, and opinions. (Though Jesus did have better hair.) So imagine Matt's astonishment when he finds out that the guy he knows as Jesus . . . isn't. He's an Imaginary Jesus: a comfortable, convenient imitation Matt has created in his own image. The real Jesus is still out there somewhere . . . and Matt is determined to find him.

Imaginary Jesus is a wild spiritual adventure like nothing you've ever read before . . . and it might bring you face-to-face with an imposter in your own life.

CP0458